ROCKETS VERSUS GRAVITY

ROCKETS VERSUS GRAVITY

RICHARD SCARSBROOK

DUNDURN
TORONTO

Editor: Shannon Whibbs
Design: Laura Boyle
Cover design and art: Laura Boyle
Additional art (ring): iStockPhoto.com/sigurcamp
Printer: Webcom

Library and Archives Canada Cataloguing in Publication

Scarsbrook, Richard, author
Rockets versus gravity / Richard Scarsbrook.

Issued in print and electronic formats.
ISBN 978-1-4597-3386-2 (paperback).--ISBN 978-1-4597-3387-9 (pdf).--
ISBN 978-1-4597-3388-6 (epub)

I. Title.
PS8587.C396R63 2016 C813'.54 C2015-908164-
C2015-908165-3

1 2 3 4 5 20 19 18 17 16

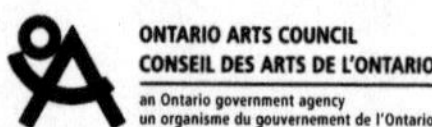

We acknowledge the support of the **Canada Council for the Arts** and the **Ontario Arts Council** for our publishing program. We also acknowledge the financial support of the **Government of Canada** through the **Canada Book Fund** and **Livres Canada Books**, and the **Government of Ontario** through the **Ontario Book Publishing Tax Credit** and the **Ontario Media Development Corporation**.

Printed and bound in Canada.

VISIT US AT

Dundurn.com | @dundurnpress | Facebook.com/dundurnpress | Pinterest.com/dundurnpress

Dundurn
3 Church Street, Suite 500
Toronto, Ontario, Canada
M5E 1M2

This book is for Bluebell
(For Evermore)

CONTENTS

Synchronicity

syn·chro·nic·i·ty

sɪŋkrəˈnɪsɪti

The simultaneous occurrence of events that appear significantly related but have no discernible causal connection.

* * *

Chaos Theory

cha·os theory

ˈkeiɒs ˈθɪə.ri

The branch of mathematics that deals with complex systems whose behaviour is highly sensitive to slight changes in conditions, so that small alterations can give rise to strikingly great consequences.

CAUSE

(PROLOGUE)

ROCKS AND ROCKETS

The flutter of a butterfly's wing.
The typhoon halfway around the world.

You linger in her doorway. Your molecules mingle.
In the sky outside, the vapour condenses.

(The sensitive dependence on initial conditions.)

If you gently brush that raindrop from her cheek, the slight cool wetness will amplify and warm, until she beckons you into her perfumed inner sanctum, where you will kneel to anoint her fragile, sacred orchid.

Then, these enraged men will lower their stones. Others will pull their fingers away from the buttons that launch the rockets.

They will hang their heads in shame and think again.

And the rockets that fly instead will escape the tyranny of gravity, will float free in space, will explore new worlds.

But, if you try to take her from behind right here in the hallway, then tomorrow the stones will pummel the earth, and the rockets will fall from the sky.

So, do what you will.

Trajectory

tra-jec-to-ry

trəˈdʒektəri

1. The path that a moving object (as a rocket) follows through space.

2. A chosen or taken course.

THE FINAL RING

Stan is sensitive to screaming. It is almost like an allergic reaction. When Sheila has a tantrum, it feels like rusty nails being driven through his temples, like crackling high-voltage wires pulling tighter and tighter around his heart.

Yet Stan's tolerance for physical pain is superheroically high.

When that axe glanced off a rock-hard knot that he couldn't see, and the rebound shattered his left knee, Stan drove himself in his pickup truck down the cratered logging road to the medical centre. He sang along to the scratchy AM radio the whole way. *"Lavender's blue, dilly dilly, Lavender's green, When I am king, dilly dilly, You shall be queen."*

When Bobby'd had a few more swigs from the flask than usual and cleaved off two of Stan's toes with the splitting awl, Stan didn't even take his boot off to look. To save Bobby's ass, he finished the last half hour of his shift without slowing down. He didn't even fill out an accident report.

So physical pain is no problem for Stan. The other guys on the crew call him the Man of Steel.

But whenever Sheila shrieks, he cringes as if he's being seared with a cattle brand.

"Gawd-dammit, Stan! Gawwwwwd-DAMMIT!" Her wail is scarcely muted by the cellphone's tiny speaker. *"Not again!*

How could you be so irresponsible? Are you a man or a child? Gawwwwwd-DAMMIT, Stan!"

The inside of the simple silver band was engraved with the words *Forever More.* Stan was pretty sure that the correct wording would have been *For Evermore,* but Sheila had insisted that her way was the correct way.

Sheila's way would *always* be the correct way. Forever More.

The first time he lost his wedding ring was on their honeymoon.

It was April 12, the same date that Yuri Gagarin became the first human to journey into outer space back in 1961. Stan had a model of Gagarin's Vostok 1 rocket, along with several other spacecraft, displayed atop the coffee table in his one-bedroom bungalow. Stan had been fascinated by space travel since he was a little kid, but guys who flunk out in grade six don't get to be to be astronauts.

On this particular April 12, Stan was sunburned, drunk, and feeling generally numb when the first ring slipped from his finger and into the blood-warm salt water. He watched it spiral downward, disappearing into the crevasses below.

He almost drowned diving for it. The salt water stung his eyes. The chemical burns from frantically groping the fire coral seared his hands. But none of these things were anything compared to the way that Stan burned and stung and choked for breath after Sheila got finished with him in the hotel room that night.

As punishment for his irresponsibility, the side trip they had planned to Cape Canaveral was cancelled, and Stan's model rockets were tossed in the trash bin by Sheila on the day she crossed the bungalow's threshold, to be replaced by her collection of Marilyn Monroe dolls.

Early the next morning, before Sheila woke from her snoring slumber and before the garbage truck began making its rounds,

Stan tiptoed outside to rescue the rockets. He hid them alongside the axes and awls and pry bars and chains inside the tool box in the back of his pickup truck. Sheila would never think to look in there.

Stan wasn't quite ready to let his rockets go.

Stan lost the second ring in a poker game.

He'd had his reservations about going with Bobby to that strip club in the city. Although the place had a classy, French-sounding name (the Ooh La La All-Nude Gentlemen's Club), it didn't have a great reputation.

The last time Stan went there, his wallet was stolen, adding insult to injury after paying twelve bucks a glass for watered-down beer and a steep cover charge to watch a raccoon-eyed single mom lumber around on stage, obviously thinking about the diapers and dishes waiting for her at home. But it had been ages since he and Sheila had been intimate, and Stan longed to see and maybe even feel some female flesh, even if he knew that the half-hearted winks and come-ons were only preludes to financial transactions.

When Bobby disappeared into one of the back rooms for a private dance, a tough-looking customer sat down at Stan's table. He wore a blue Toronto Maple Leafs jersey with the name SPRINGTHORPE spelled across the back in white iron-on letters.

"Wanna play some cards?" this gentleman asked.

"Sure," Stan said, without thinking much about it.

After three hands, Stan didn't have enough cash left to pay for his twelve-dollar beer, so the slick sunnuvabitch took Stan's ring instead.

Stan removed all of the model rockets from inside the toolbox in the back of his pickup truck, and he exchanged them at the local pawnshop for enough cash to replace the ring before Sheila ever noticed that it was missing. At the last minute, he decided to keep the replica of the Saturn V that carried the Apollo 11 astronauts to the moon, and he still received enough money to pay the local jeweller.

It was a bittersweet victory for Stan.

Stan lost the third ring while wrestling with a logjam in the flume.

He hadn't had time to pull on his gauntlet gloves or even to grab a pry bar, and as he grappled with the log that had turned sideways and caused the blockage, his fingers got caught between its scaly bark and the rough-sawn head of another log. He pulled as if his life depended on it (because it did), and in the end he managed to keep all of his fingers. In exchange, he gave up some knuckle skin, some blood, and his replacement wedding ring.

By the time Sheila was finished with him that night, Stan almost wished he'd gone down with the rumbling stampede of logs. She banished him from the house, pulled down the blinds, and locked the doors.

He curled up inside the cab of his truck, but he couldn't sleep for the ringing in his ears. He switched on the radio, and the voice inside the speaker informed him that "Today in history, January 28, 1986, all seven crew members of the NASA space shuttle *Challenger* were killed when the spacecraft broke apart seventy-three seconds into its flight."

Stan cried for the rest of the night.

And now Stan's ears are ringing again as Sheila screams at him through the cellphone speaker, *"Gawd-dammit, Stan! Gawwwwwd-fucking-DAMMIT! That's THREE FUCKING RINGS! How could you lose THREE FUCKING WEDDING RINGS?"*

It is actually *four* rings, but Stan isn't about to correct Sheila. When she pauses to refill her lungs, Stan simply says, "I won't need a replacement."

"And just what the hell do you mean by THAT?"

The forest floor is cool against Stan's neck. His back is cushioned by the fallen leaves. Above him, branches reach up like skeletal fingertips into the lavender-blue sky.

The chainsaw smells like burnt oil; its engine sputters on the ground beside him, finally stalling.

The spatters on the trees blink faintly in the day's dying light. The shimmer on the dark pool of blood turns matte as it is sucked down into the dark forest soil.

In his soft but rumbling voice, Stan finally says, "I also lost the hand the ring was attached to, Sheila."

With the hand that is still attached to his body, the last thing that Stan does in his life is switch off the phone.

And then there is silence.

Sweet, sweet, beautiful silence.

And there are stars.

For evermore.

BLINK

Clementine was fond of that red light, blinking gently atop the radio tower in the distance. She found it reassuring, like the tolling of the church bells, which she had heard for her entire life; or maybe it was more like the heartbeat of a sleeping lover, which she hoped she might someday feel throbbing against her skin.

Light on, light off. Light on, light off.

From the musty-smelling cot in her tiny bedroom, she could see the red light pulsing, amplified by the warped glass of the small single window, which was not masked with curtains or with blinds.

"Can't we even get some cheap venetian blinds, Mother?" she had pleaded. "People can see me undressing through the window!"

"*What* people?" her mother had scolded. "There isn't another farm for five miles. Vanity is a sin, young lady."

Leave it to her mother to interpret her modesty as vanity.

So she had become accustomed to the red light winking at her from atop the radio tower through the uncovered window. Its repetitive glow lulled her to sleep every night

Light on, light off. Light on, light off.

Everything in the farmhouse was over a hundred years old, passed down from one generation to the next; even her own name: Clementine. The other girls at school, the ones with their matching boutique-store jeans and purses with brand names displayed on huge brass tags, the ones who constantly chirped "OMG!" and "Like, totally!" all had post-modern names like TV sitcom characters: Shaniqua and Kaylee, Makayla and Amberlindzy. Clementine was stuck with her great-grandmother's recycled name and the feeling that she belonged in another time.

When she concentrated on that blinking red light, Clementine could ignore the sounds of loose shingles flapping in the breeze overhead and the scratching of mice inside the walls; she could ignore the faint smell of fertilizer and insecticide wafting in from the fields outside; she could ignore the bearlike snarl of her father snoring in the adjacent room.

But sometimes the red light wasn't calming. It didn't always lull her. Sometimes it was stimulating. Sometimes it throbbed.

Light on, light off. Light on, light off.

On summer nights like this one, when the air was heavy and humid and smelled like a sweat-glazed farmhand, she would kick off the abrasive wool blanket, and she would allow her fingers to snake down between her legs, into the slippery wet space beneath her thick tangle of pubic hair, and she would stroke herself to the rhythm of that pulsing red light.

Light on, light off. Light on, light off.

As the only girl in the family, at least she had her own bedroom; her four older brothers shared a single room not much bigger than hers. She imagined that such nocturnal releases were nearly impossible for her brothers to enjoy undetected.

She found it difficult to believe the popular implication that boys needed it more than girls; she needed it almost every night, and the need built up inside her during every minute of every day that slowly ticked past.

Light on, light off. Light on, light off.

Then her father allowed them to put up that billboard on the edge of their property beside the concession road, right between Clementine's window and the radio tower. In exchange for ten percent of the advertising revenue, Clementine's father sold away her view of the pulsing red light.

Now all she has to look at in her room at night is the peeling wallpaper, which was pasted up by her great-grandmother, the original Clementine, back in the days when the house was new, and working the land was noble and profitable — God's own work.

The current, living Clementine looks at the wallpaper now, with its repeating diagonal pattern of unintentionally vaginal-looking pink orchids and phallic purple irises.

Or maybe it wasn't so unintentional, she thinks. *Maybe, behind closed doors, those Victorians were a lot sexier than they would have us believe. Maybe they were just more subtle about it.*

Maybe my great-grandmother did exactly what I'm going to do now. Maybe these miniature erections and moist vulva petals helped get her going.

Clementine has to bite her lip, flip over, and press her face into her earth-scented pillow to prevent herself from crying out loud, from screaming the name of a lover whom she doesn't yet know.

She can no longer see it, but she knows that the light is still there, shining, pulsing, radiating.

Light on, light off. Light on, light off.

Aleksander almost enjoys it when they pick fights with him. It is always so predictable. In a way, it is reassuring. It reminds him that the universe follows a certain set of rules: rules of geometry, rules of physics, rules of mathematics.

It is more or less the same fight every time, which is why he always wins.

One of them will inevitably saunter across the parking lot, wearing the standard uniform: the unlaced boots, the faded blue jeans, the untucked plaid lumberjack shirt, the varsity team jacket with the purple felt body and the white leather sleeves.

"Hey, faggot!" the tough guy will bray. "You like sucking cocks? Wanna suck mine?" Or some other variation on this theme.

Most of the other guys in purple-and-white team jackets will laugh along. One or two will *pretend* to laugh. And at least one, usually the guy standing farthest from the potential altercation, will not laugh at all, will not even pretend to laugh. Standard and predictable pack dynamics.

Today's declaration of war is, "So, weirdo. You like black leather, eh? You a perv or something?"

Aleksander doesn't stand up. Not yet. It's best not to seem too eager at first. Between the thumb and index finger of his right hand, Aleksander casually twists the simple silver ring that encircles his left-hand ring finger.

Clockwise, counter-clockwise. Clockwise, counter-clockwise.

"Yep," he finally says, "I *do* like black leather. And it appears that you like *white* leather. Which I suppose begs the question: Are *you* a pervert? Are you a white-leather pervert?"

"I guess you haven't been going to this school for very long," Mr. Team Jacket says, striding toward Aleksander, opening and closing his fingers like Venus flytraps. "Do you know who I am?"

"Well, I don't go to this school — or to any other school, actually — but I've observed that the sleeves of your jacket are embroidered with the words *captain* and *football*, so I'm going to deduce that your name is Captain Football. That's some very pretty embroidery, by the way."

Captain Football is standing right in front of Aleksander now, his belt buckle level with Aleksander's nose. The scent of cologne wafts downward.

"So, answer my question, assboy," Captain Football demands. "Me and the boys wanna know: Is your black leather some kinda *feetish*? Are you some kind of sicko?"

"I believe that you mean to say 'The boys and I,' not 'Me and the boys,'" Aleksander says, rising from the concrete parking divider. "And it's pronounced *fett*-ish, not *feet*-ish."

"Oh. Sorry. *Fett*-ish," Mr. Team Jacket says, taking a step forward. "You got a *pain* fetish, gimp? I hope so, 'cause I'm gonna ..."

One of two things will happen at this point. If the guy is a hockey or basketball player, he will lunge forward and throw a punch at Aleksander's face; but if his jacket has *Football* embroidered on its white leather sleeve, he will run at Aleksander and try to tackle him, to force him onto the ground.

In the Punching Scenario, Aleksander will step out of the radius of the assailant's punch, and as soon as the fist has sailed past his face, he will step back into the radius, just close enough to smash the attacker's nose with an immediate counterpunch.

Step out, lean in.

Then, as his opponent staggers backward from the blow, sometimes swinging wildly on his way down, Aleksander will deliver a quick, hard kick between his aggressor's legs, which usually sends the guy tumbling backward onto the pavement. About seven times out of ten, a tailbone fracture results from the fall.

Step out, lean in.

In the Tackling Scenario (which is about to take place here), the manoeuvres are even simpler. As the guy barrels toward him, Aleksander merely steps out of the path of the attacker's charge at the very last minute. His opponent will sometimes be bent forward far enough that Aleksander can deliver a spin-kick to the guy's balls from behind as he passes; but if the guy isn't leaning into it enough (or has very small balls), Aleksander cracks the guy's tailbone with the steel toe of his black boot instead.

Step out, lean in.

In this scenario, the broken nose will be delivered from above, *after* the other guy hits the ground. And then, if Aleksander missed them on the first pass, he will retroactively kick his opponent in the testicles.

Step out, lean in.

It's not about being tough. It's not about being brave.

It's about geometry. It's about physics. It's about mathematics.

Trajectory. Circumference. Deflection. Timing.

Step out, lean in.

The equation has always added up to this: Aleksander will remain standing; his assailant will not. Aleksander will remain uninjured, except maybe for some bruised knuckles, while his attacker will possess at least one (but usually all three) of the following modifications to his physiology: a broken nose, a broken tailbone, and traumatically injured testicles.

Now Captain Football is curled up in a quivering fetal ball on the cold, cracked pavement, coughing up vomit and blood. His upper lip is split, and his nose is certainly broken; Aleksander felt the cartilage snap against his knuckles. Aleksander landed his single punch and two kicks with the accuracy of sniper's bullets; this one won't be able to sit comfortably or blow his nose without pain for some time.

Predictably, a few of the buddies run over to aid their fallen comrade. A few others, the ones who were laughing the loudest less than a minute ago, advance on Aleksander.

"You're dead, asshole!"

"So fucking dead!"

This is the point at which Aleksander reaches into his black leather jacket and then snaps open the switchblade.

The advance halts.

Aleksander stands with his feet wide apart, his knees bent, his arms stretched wide, as if he's about to leap up into the misty air and fly away. The blade in his right hand glints amber from the sodium-vapour parking lot lights overhead.

Captain Football limps away with his brothers in arms. One of them calls out, "You're gonna die, buddy."

Aleksander says, "No, I will not."

As they retreat toward a shining Dodge pickup truck, another teammate says, "We'll find you, gimp."

Aleksander says, "No, you will not."

Another, who is helping to lift Captain Football over the tail-gate, adds, "We know where you live, fucker."

Aleksander says, "No, you do not."

He doesn't lower his arms or move his feet until the pickup truck has roared away, its red tail lights vanishing into the foggy air. Then Aleksander plunges headlong into the mist, the last figure to vanish from the scene, as always.

Step out, lean in.

No matter how close she stands to her tiny bedroom window, from whatever angle she looks, Clementine's view of the outside world is now filled with the billboard.

The first advertisement to go up was for a local insurance agency. Beneath the company's logo was a huge photograph of the office's "Number One Sales Agent," with her pimples and lady-moustache expertly airbrushed away. Beside her portrait, the words:

Brooklynn Tripp
Broker

One night, while Clementine was sleeping, someone with a can of black spray paint climbed the billboard's tall iron frame and added the following:

Brooklynn Tripped and Broker NECK!

Clementine gasped when she saw it through her bedroom window in the morning, and she giggled when she told her mother about it at breakfast.

Her mother reached across the table and slapped her face. "Vandalism is not funny," she said. "Defacing the property of others is a sin."

Well, technically, it was a sin to *covet* the property of others, not to *deface* it. Clementine was about to correct her mother on this point but then decided against it. She wasn't in the mood to offer the other cheek.

"Besides," her mother added, "they pay us a few dollars a month for the land that billboard's on, and Lord knows, we need all the help we can get."

From his seat at the kitchen table, Clementine's father rasped, "I'm doin' the best I can, woman."

"Lord knows," her mother said, to nobody in particular. "Lord knows."

Her father wasn't sure about what to do next. Should he call the police? The municipality? The billboard company? So he went to seek the counsel of Pastor Okonjo.

After praying, consulting the scriptures, and meditating on the issue, the pastor decided that it would be best to have the commercial advertising removed from the billboard altogether and to have church-approved messages pasted up there instead.

The pastor reasoned that, because the billboard was strategically located along the concession road that led to the church, many lost and wayward souls might be saved by the billboard's divine placement; and, although Clementine's father would lose his small cut of the advertising revenue, he would surely be compensated a hundredfold in Heaven for helping to communicate the Word of the Lord to His followers.

So, in letters four feet tall, the next message on the billboard read simply:

JESUS is COMING!

Pastor Okonjo was pleased. That would put a few extra bodies in the pews and a few extra dollars on the collection plate.

Within two nights, though, the message had become:

JESUS is COMING!
Look Busy!

Clementine's father went to see Pastor Okonjo right away. The pastor, after once again praying, consulting the scriptures, and meditating on the issue, decreed that Clementine's father would climb the billboard with a can of white spray paint and obliterate the offending words. The vandal would see that his blasphemy was being actively resisted, and the coward would move on to other victims with less pure resolve.

Clementine's father did as he was instructed. He eradicated the offensive black words, the white paint jetting from the can with hissing, evangelical fury.

Yet, within another two nights, the message became:

JESUS is COMING!
Hide the booze!

Clementine's father did not go to the pastor this time. This was personal now.

He climbed the frame again, and, with dignity and fervour, he once again sprayed good clean white over the offensive back letters.

Then, for the next week, Clementine's father sat on the front porch at night with his twelve-gauge shotgun laid across his lap. This was his God-given property, and he would protect it from evil. He rocked back and forth, levelling his steely gaze at the billboard across the field, waiting to see if the vandal would have the audacity to reappear. He would not forgive those who trespassed against him.

By the evening of the seventh day, her father decided that the danger had passed, and he eventually came inside to watch reruns of *7th Heaven* on TV.

Clementine stayed up late that night, gazing through her small window, hoping to catch a glimpse of the elusive spray-paint hoodlum. He never appeared, though, and eventually she lay back on her bed and, surrounded by dancing purple phalluses and gyrating pink vulvas, stirred her whirlpool until her desires were sucked under and drowned once again.

On the morning of the eighth day, the message on the billboard read:

JESUS is COMING!
Oh god, oh god, oh god!

* * *

Now it is Sunday, and today at church, the parishioners are particularly incensed that the vandal didn't spell "God" with a capital *G*, and most are far too flustered to even mention the … the … *connotation* … in the vandal's most recent blasphemy.

Pastor Okonjo, in one of his more rousing sermons, intones that the vandal has declared Holy War, and that reaction from the church will be swift and just.

Within a week, the billboard will have a new message:

JUDGMENT DAY is COMING

No one will have the gall to mess with *that* message, the pastor reckons. No one will have anything funny to say about *that.*

And, as it turns out, no one does. The vandal will not strike again.

In the shadowy back left corner of the church, a young man in a black leather jacket sits quietly in an otherwise unoccupied pew, casually twisting the simple silver ring that encircles his left-hand ring finger.

Clockwise, counter-clockwise. Clockwise, counter-clockwise.

No one in the agitated congregation seems to notice him, no one but Clementine, that is.

"Mother," she asks at the end of the service, "are we staying for the after-service luncheon?"

"No," her mother says, shooting an icy glance at Clementine's father. "It's cheaper for us to eat at home."

"Well," Clementine says, all saccharine sweetness, "would it be all right if I stayed behind to help the ladies pour the tea?"

Of course this is all right with her mother! She wants to see Clementine kept busy. *The Devil makes work for idle hands.*

As soon as she sees her parents drive away in their pickup truck, Clementine walks across the street to where the young man in the leather jacket sits on a park bench beside the cenotaph.

"So, you're new to the church, aren't you?"

"I'm pretty familiar to the church, actually," he says, pausing to light a cigarette. "But if you mean that my presence is unfamiliar inside this particular building, then yes, you are correct."

Slender tendrils of smoke curl around his wrist like ghostly serpents.

She asks him, "Is that black spray paint on your fingers?"

"Is that a halo hovering over your head?"

She blushes a little. "No. Definitely not."

"Good," he says. "Saints are boring. Most of them, anyway."

"You know a lot of saints, do you?"

"All of 'em. Every single one."

He holds the lit cigarette out toward her.

"I don't smoke," she says.

"Ah. Not a sinner, then."

"I don't think smoking's a sin," she says. "Spray painting graffiti on billboards probably isn't, either. But I'm not sure that doing either one is good for your health in the long run."

"I was just being funny. Jesus doesn't mind. Neither does Brooklyn Tripp. They've both got a sense of humour."

"How do you know that?"

He takes a long drag and then exhales white smoke. "I just do." He raises the cigarette to his lips once again. "Want to sit?"

She does.

Her heart throbs. It's like he's from another time. Not from the days of her namesake great-grandmother, but not from this era, either. He is from someplace in between, a more liberated age, a place in time where Clementine wants to be.

"You should probably get some blinds for your bedroom window," he says.

Clementine's breath catches in her throat.

"Somebody might see you," he says. "Somebody might start believing in love at first sight."

Clementine's mouth drops open. Could he see her in her bedroom from his perch upon the billboard? Clementine knows that she should find this weird. She should find this creepy. But she doesn't. She finds it stimulating. She finds it sexy. She is filled with want. "You've got a beautiful mouth," he says.

She is drawn to the calm confidence in his cool blue eyes. She wants to reach out and touch his sculptured-stone jaw. She longs to lean forward and kiss his round, moist lips.

She hears herself saying, "Thank you."

"You aren't going to run away now?"

"No."

"Aren't you afraid that I might be dangerous?"

"A little bit."

"I'm only dangerous to those who intend to cause harm. And you don't intend to harm anyone, do you?"

"No."

As he raises his smoke once again, his silver ring glints in the afternoon sunlight.

"Is that a wedding ring?" Clementine asks. "Are you a married man?"

He tosses the cigarette aside. "Nah. I bought this ring at the pawn shop right up the street from here. I always like to pick up a little souvenir from each town I pass through."

He twists the ring between the thumb and index finger of his right hand.

Clockwise, counter-clockwise. Clockwise, counter-clockwise.

Finally, it pops over the bulbous knuckle of his left-hand ring finger.

"The guy at the pawnshop said that some lumberjack — named Bobby, he thought — brought the ring in a while back. The guy had found it wedged into one of the seams of a log flume, of all places, so Bobby, if that was his name, traded it for a pewter whiskey flask. That was the story, anyway. Everything has a story. Every single thing."

He offers the ring to Clementine. She takes it and reads aloud the inscription engraved inside the simple loop: "*Forever More.*"

"I think that the engraver might have made a mistake, though," he says. "I think it should read 'For Evermore.'"

"What's the difference?" Clementine wonders.

"There's a profound difference," he says.

She extends her arm to hand the ring back to him, but he says, "Keep it. It's yours."

Clementine knows that the ladylike thing would be to protest, but she doesn't. She closes her fingers around the ring and holds it against her chest.

"So," she says, leaning toward him, "did you enjoy watching me sleeping?"

She is surprised when his face flushes. He looks away for a moment before he says, "I wasn't watching. I just happened to see." Then he grins a sly, mischievous little smile. "And you weren't sleeping."

Clementine's jaw drops open again.

"It's the most beautiful thing I've seen in a long, long time," he says. "It's the first honest moment I've seen in this town. It's the first thing that anyone has done that wasn't disguising itself as something else."

Clementine knows that she should get up and walk away, run away even, but those eyes. Those lips. He generates some strange kind of gravity that holds her in his orbit.

For the seventh Sunday in a row, Clementine volunteers to stay behind to help at the after-service luncheon.

In the cab of the pickup truck, Clementine's mother sighs. "Our girl is growing up."

Her father nods as he steers the pickup around the ruts in the laneway. "She's been a woman for some time now, Pearl. You were younger than she is when we got together."

Pearl turns on the bench seat, reaches out to pat her husband's thigh. "I'm sorry if I'm hard sometimes, Darryl. I do love you, y'know."

Darryl grins shyly. "I know, Pearl. I know."

He brings the truck to a gentle halt in front of the old farmhouse. It rocks back and forth on its rusty springs.

At the same moment, in the forest behind the cenotaph across the street from the church, Clementine is leaning back against the trunk of an ancient tree, entwined with Aleksander, rocking back and forth at a similar frequency. The silver ring lies between her breasts, on the same slender chain that carries her crucifix.

This is the first time that they have coupled like this. Aleksander has pleasured her in other ways: spiralling his dextrous tongue against her sweet spot as she lies back on the spongy ground with her legs spread wide, fingering her from behind as she stands with one leg wrapped around a smooth-barked tree trunk.

But this time is different. It's beyond anything else. Clementine feels untethered from time, free in space. Each stroke fills her with a pulse of warm red light

Light on, light off. Light on, light off.

Light on.

Light on.

Light ON.

They collapse against the body of the tree, bonded together by shared heat and mingled sweat and the dénouement of mutual breathing.

When Clementine whispers, "Oh, God," she means it. She is a believer once again.

"Well, well," a voice rasps from over Aleksander's shoulder, "what have we here?"

Aleksander spins around. Clementine pushes her dress back down below her knees.

It takes Aleksander a moment to recognize Captain Football and his posse; they have replaced their purple-and-white team jackets with dark, Sunday-best suits.

This will not be predictable. There is a new variable that changes the equation.

"Run, Clementine," he whispers in her ear. "Run. Now. Go."

Clementine runs. By the time she bursts out of the forest, Captain Football and his minions will have repaid Aleksander's single punch and two kicks many, many times over.

Aleksander's internal organs rupture as Captain Football delivers kick after kick after kick. He rages, "Stop smiling, you fucking freak!"

But Aleksander continues smiling. A destiny more terrible than this one has been averted.

One by one, the minions disappear. The last one to turn away says, "Fuck, man, he's had enough!"

But the kicker keeps kicking, long after Aleksander's smile has frozen on his face.

Clementine turns the plastic crank to open the cheap venetian blinds, and she peers out through her tiny bedroom window. The workers are preparing to paste a new billboard over the previous one.

Her father figured that he had better start allowing the commercial advertising again, with another mouth to feed and all. That ten percent revenue would buy a lot of baby food. Maybe some of it could even go into a college fund or something like that.

When Clementine could hide it no longer and the time came to reveal her pregnancy, she had expected her mother to strike her over and over again, to scream the word *bastard*, to sermonize about the "sin of carnal knowledge outside the sanctity of marriage." But Clementine's mother just reached for her knitting needles and said, "Well, I'd best start knitting you some baby clothes, then."

Maybe her mother reckoned that Clementine had already been punished enough.

When Clementine was subpoenaed to testify at the trial, she couldn't answer a single question without breaking down in tears. Fortunately, several of Captain Football's former teammates had come forward, and the prosecutor was able to convict him; not for murder, but for a reduced charge of manslaughter, with a sentence of the minimum four years.

Captain Football's father could afford to hire a very expensive defence attorney. In this world, nothing is ever really an eye for an eye, and Clementine cried over this realization for a very long time.

The teammates who came forward were made to suffer. They were called "rats," and there were sidewalk whispers and barroom shouts about the heinous crime of "snitching on a teammate." Clementine cried over this injustice, too.

Whenever a member of their church congregation cast judgmental eyes upon her from their pew bench perches, whispering words like "harlot" and "bastard" in Old Testament tones, Clementine's tears would gush yet again.

But now her cheeks are finally dry.

Clementine cradles the child against her chest. She has named him Aleksander, after his father. He's a good baby. He never cries.

On the billboard outside her bedroom window, Clementine watches the letters disappear, one by one:

JUDGMENT DAY is COMING

It came. It went. And she and her son were allowed to survive.

By the time the new advertisement has been pasted up, night is overtaking day. And behind the billboard, at the top of the radio tower in the distance, the red light is gently blinking. She cannot see it from here, but Clementine still tries to find it reassuring.

Light on, light off. Light on, light off.

One day she will follow that blinking light away from this place.

THE CODE

It's the pre-game warm-up, and the whole team's got the jitters. Even me.

This is the most people I've seen inside the Faireville Memorial Arena in a long, long time. On the edges of the bench seats that surround the ice, they are perched like predatory birds, their sharp eyes tracking the skaters as they circle their zones and lob pucks at the net during the pre-game skate. Everyone is crushed right together, shoulder to shoulder, thigh against thigh. They're all singing along with the arena anthems blasting from the low-fidelity loudspeakers, punctuated by the occasional scream of "WHOOOOOOOOOO!"

Wheelie Koontz, the kid who sets up the PA system when the principal lectures us in the gym at school, is up there in the DJ booth. Wheelie can't play hockey himself, or any other sport, because he was born with spina bifida, and he's bound to a wheelchair. He sure knows how to get a pre-game crowd fired up, though. Right now, he's playing that song by Stompin' Tom Connors. You know, the one that goes, *"The good ol' hockey game is the best game you can name."*

The arena roars with the voices singing along; well, more like shouting along, really. There's not a lot of melody or harmony in the collective voices.

Before that, Wheelie played the one about the guy wanting his boy to play in the big league. And before that, it was the one by, um, what're they called again? Gawd, my memory sucks. Oh, yeah, it's The Tragically Hip. Yeah, that's it. You know, the one about Bill Barilko scoring the goal that won the Leafs the Stanley Cup.

It's tough to be a Leafs fan, isn't it? I mean, they haven't won a Stanley Cup since 1967, which is way before I was even born. Wheelie says that Toronto Maple Leafs fans are masochists, which I think means that they secretly enjoy all the suffering that the Leafs cause them. The Leafs give them something to holler about, a reason to let out some of their anger over the bigger things that might be eating at them.

About a third of the hockey fans in Faireville root for the Leafs; all you have to do is count the number of blue-and-white jerseys in the crowd. Toronto is the closest Canadian city to Faireville, and this is the main reason why my dad cheers for them: loyalty to the "local team." Another reason why Dad supports the Leafs is that his own dad rooted for the Montreal Canadiens, at least until the old man left home and never came back when my dad was nine years old. Dad has hated the Montreal Canadiens ever since, and Leafs/Habs games are weighted with more importance in our household than federal elections or rocket launches.

Me? Well, I just can't get behind a team that keeps trading away its promising younger players for old goats who, you know, got forty points one season five years ago before blowing out a knee. And I just can't get past the fact that the Leafs sell all their tickets to Bay Street lawyers and stockbrokers and bankers who write off the tickets as a "business expense," and then they spend most of the game in the bar, or they're on their damned phones the whole time the game's being played, while the real fans can't afford to buy tickets at all and only get to holler at the Leafs through the TVs in their rec rooms. I haven't shared any of these opinions with my dad, though. When he's got the game on at home, I pretend to be happy when the Leafs score.

About another third of the townies root for the Red Wings, because they're actually the closest NHL team to Faireville. They play just across the Detroit River, which is only a forty-five-minute drive across the county from Faireville. Not everyone is so patriotic that they feel they have to get behind a Canadian team; hell, a few guys around here even cheer for the Flyers and the Bruins. My dad thinks that these fans are traitors to their country, and he doesn't mind telling them so when he's watching a game on the big screens at one of the local bars.

Just about everyone else in the arena roots for Montreal, because back a couple hundred years ago, the Brits kicked a bunch of the French out of what's now Quebec, and they settled just up the road from Faireville in Rivière Lévesque, a village that isn't big enough to have its own hockey team. I guess the Leveckers (that's what we call them here in Faireville) still feel some connection to their former countrymen who stayed in Montreal; most of the Leveckers still speak French at home. Of all of the barroom fistfights that my dad has had over the years, most of them were with Hab-fan Leveckers.

Me? Well, I secretly root for the Ottawa Senators, who are pretty much despised by Red Wings, Canadiens, and Leafs fans alike. Why the Senators? Because once, when I was just a little kid, my dad drove me to Ottawa in his truck to go see a Senators game, and it's still one of the best memories I've got.

When the Senators started back up as an NHL team, they played at the tiny Ottawa Civic Centre, because I guess they hadn't earned enough money to build an NHL-size arena yet. Dad was running up to Ottawa to bring some supplies back to the factory anyway, and last-minute game tickets at the Civic Centre were pretty cheap, so he figured, "Why not take the kid to see a game?"

Even though the Senators were beaten four-two by the Bruins that night, my dad and I had fun together. It was the last time I can remember him smiling at me, actually. It was the last time that he punched me just for sport; you know, on the shoulder, just for fun.

Sometime during the third period, one of the Senators players challenged one of the Bruins to a fight for chopping one of his teammates on the ankle with his stick. The Senator lost the fight and skated off with a bloody nose, but my father stood up and cheered for the guy as he left the ice with a towel over his face.

"That's the stuff, Aaron," Dad said to me. "That's the Code. You gotta stand up for your teammates when someone does them wrong. You gotta stand up for yourself, too. Even if you lose the battle, you win the war. Understand?"

I told him that I did.

Then Dad got all teary-eyed, like he sometimes does when he's drunk, and he reached into the inside pocket of his parka and plucked out a simple silver ring.

"This is for you, kiddo. I won it fair and square in a poker game, so it's a winner's ring. It's a lucky ring. I want you to have it."

The ring was engraved on the inside with the words *Forever More*. Even on my thickest finger the ring was loose, but I wore it anyway.

We turned right around after the game and drove the eight hours back to Faireville, because Dad couldn't afford for us to stay the night in a hotel room. We ran out of gas on the way home, though; in the middle of the night, in the dead of winter, in the middle of nowhere. That part was less fun. It did not put Dad in a very good mood.

The Ottawa Senators set three NHL records during that inaugural season, by the way: the longest home losing streak (eleven games), the longest road losing streak (thirty-eight!), and the fewest road wins in a season (one). Still, I started rooting for them back then. My dad says that I'm a sucker for the underdog, and I guess that's true. And the Senators did eventually get better.

The team that I play for, the Faireville Blue Flames, has a similar record to the first-year Senators, by the way. We are in dead-last place in the league, and we are about to play the Gasberg Pipefitters, who are so far ahead of every other team in the league that, even if they lost the rest of their games this season, they would *still* be the champions.

Now Wheelie Koontz is playing the song about the guy wanting to drive the Zamboni. I actually drove the Zamboni once, when Earl, the arena manager, got too drunk to park it himself after an old-timer's game went into triple overtime. Driving the Zamboni is really not a big deal; it's like steering an oversized, top-heavy lawn tractor around. A Zamboni is not exactly a "Powerful-yet-Nimble Driving Machine" (a phrase I borrowed from the rinkside advertisement for Gasberg Exotic Sports Cars). Still, the capacity crowd is singing (well, screaming) that they want to drive the Zamboni, too, when the lyrics are overwhelmed by a collective scream of "WHOOOOOOOOOO!" as Keegan Thrush steps onto the ice.

A bunch of girls from our high school, their faces painted purple and gold, wave a spray-painted bedsheet banner that reads KEEGAN THRUSH IS #1!!!!! They drool over his architecturally perfect face, and they write poems in English class detailing his sky-blue eyes, wavy dark hair, strong cheekbones, and square jaw. The high-tech body armour beneath his jersey makes him look even more like a mythical warrior. When he points the end of his expensive composite stick toward their section of the stands, the girls all scream orgasmically, the heat of their bodies almost melting the purple-and-gold makeup from their faces. Their hero has acknowledged them! Oh my *gawd*!

Purple and gold are Gasberg's team colours, by the way. Our team colours are blue and silver.

Even though Keegan lives in Faireville, he is eligible to play for the Gasberg team because he goes to school there. His parents send him to Eagle Crest Preparatory College, the twenty-five-thousand-dollar-a-year private high school in the city. Unlike most people in Faireville, they can afford to send Keegan to Eagle Crest, because Keegan's dad owns Gasberg Exotic Sports Cars; he also has controlling interests in a number of other "exotic" businesses, like the "exotic" dancers at the Ooh La La All-Nude Gentlemen's Club, as well as the "exotic" substances dealt in its back room.

It would normally raise a lot of eyebrows that Ramsay Thrush drives a Maserati in a town where everyone else drives ten-year-old pickup trucks and Honda Civics, but since Ramsay makes a big show of donating money to every local charity and cause, most people turn a blind eye to his more questionable enterprises. With their good eyes, they choose to see him as an upstanding civic leader and admirable philanthropist, as long as he keeps that messy stuff in the city, where it belongs.

Normally, Keegan would be considered a traitor to his hometown for playing for Gasberg, but somehow the adults of Faireville all love Keegan, too. Keegan lives with his parents in one of the lace-trimmed estates in Victoria Park, in the very home where Prime Minister Abbott slept one night, so Keegan's got the please-and-thank-you manners of Faireville's tea-and-cookie elite. This makes the Faireville moms believe that he's Ideal Husband Material for their daughters.

Meanwhile, the Faireville dads believe that Keegan will be going to the Big Show one of these days, and they're all itching for the day he scores his first NHL goal on TV, so they can say to whoever is sitting beside them in their basement rec room, "I watched him play his final game at the Faireville Memorial Arena. I knew it then. I knew it then."

The ref blows the whistle for the game to begin, but none of the players can hear it for the noise of the screaming crowd. So the ref waves his arms in the air and blows the whistle again, so loudly this time that his cheeks puff out and turn purple.

Keegan Thrush skates to centre ice for the opening faceoff, wearing a confident grin like one of those cowboy heroes in the 1950s serials that they play late at night on the public television channel (which is one of three stations we get on the tinfoil antennas on our ancient TV). There is a good reason for Keegan's confident grin: the Gasberg Pipefitters' previous game against the Brownton Buttermilkers.

The Buttermilkers have got intimidating-looking black-and-gold jerseys, like the Boston Bruins. They've also got the most terrible name in the history of hockey. *The Brownton Buttermilkers* sounds like the title of one of those pastel-covered paperback novels that my mother likes to read: *The Southern Saffron Soufflé Sisterhood* or *The Peterborough Puddin' Pie Protectorate.* Despite their less-than-threatening name, though, the Buttermilkers are a hell of a better hockey team than we are, the second-best in the league. And just last week, Keegan Thrush scored *ten unassisted goals* on them.

Think about that for a minute. *Ten* goals. *Unassisted.* Ten goals, all by himself. Against an entire team of decent players.

To put this feat in perspective, the highest number of *points* ever scored in a NHL game was ten, by the Toronto Maple Leafs'

Darryl Sittler, versus the Boston Bruins. Sittler scored six goals and contributed four assists. It has never happened again since, and probably never will.

Darryl Sittler got six goals and four helpers. Keegan Thrush scored *ten goals.*

Now, I understand that the Wheatfield Major Junior Hockey League is not exactly the NHL, and that the Brownton Buttermilkers are not the Boston Bruins. But still, against our pathetic team it's possible that Keegan will score *eleven* goals tonight.

This is what everyone is hoping to see. Everyone wants to see Keegan Thrush set yet *another* league record.

Nobody is here to cheer for their pitiful home team. Everyone in town has crammed into the Faireville Memorial Arena to watch Keegan Thrush single-handedly destroy the Faireville Blue Flames.

Everyone but my dad, that is. He may be the only person in Faireville who isn't in love with Keegan Thrush.

"You should drop the gloves with that gawd-damned pretty-boy traitor," Dad said through gritted teeth as we walked to the arena. "Are you wearing your lucky ring?"

"Yep. I'm wearing it." The ring is too tight for me now, but I still wear it when I'm playing hockey. Dad takes it personally when I don't, and, well, he's not a lot of fun to be around when he takes things personally.

"You should put it right in that little prick's eye!" Dad yelped. "Fuckin' show 'im, that little panty-wearing rich boy. It's the Code, Aaron. You always gotta live by the Code."

Keegan never drops the gloves, though. No matter what you say to him, no matter what you do, he always just smiles and skates away. One of his teammates usually charges in to do the fighting for him; they can't have the guy who scores ninety percent of their goals getting injured in a brawl.

In his own hockey-playing days, my dad was like Keegan Thrush in one way: he always skated away from the altercation with a smile on his face. But that was after leaving his opponent's body, and some of his blood, and often a few of his teeth, splattered and scattered on the ice. When Dad played for the Blue Flames, he was known as Pauly "The Pummeller" Springthorpe. He still holds the all-time record for penalty minutes in the Wheatfield League.

One of the managers at the Krispy Green Pickle factory was a fan of "Old Time Hockey," and he had the entire library of *Don Cherry's Rock 'Em Sock 'Em Hockey* videos at home to prove it; so when Dad hung up his skates after going undrafted in his final Junior year, he was invited to go to work on the jar-filling line at Krispy Green.

During the scheduled breaks at the factory, Dad had a habit of leaving his position on the line for a half-hour or more to smoke his hand-rolled cigarettes, or sometimes to have a snort or two from the mickey of Scotch he kept inside the pocket of his coveralls. The problem was, the scheduled breaks were only supposed to last for fifteen minutes, and the rest of the guys on the line had to wait (and do nothing and therefore make the factory no money) whenever my dad was late returning.

When the afternoon-shift foreman called Dad out in front of the other guys, Dad transformed once again into the Pummeller. He left the old man lying on the concrete factory floor with a broken nose, a row of smashed teeth, lacerations on his face where his glasses had shattered, and three cracked ribs. ("That last part wasn't my fault!" Dad pleaded in court. "He hit the conveyor-belt motor on the way down!")

While he was on the ice, wearing his Faireville Blue Flames jersey, Dad would have served five minutes in the penalty box for fighting, or, if he really beat the crap out of a guy, maybe an extra ten and a game misconduct. For the incident on the factory floor, while wearing his factory-issued coveralls, he was punished with a minimum sentence of five years in prison for aggravated assault.

After he served his time, nobody offered to give Dad his job back at the factory, and he hasn't had one since.

Anyway, thanks to my dad's reputation, I'm usually obliged once a game to go out and fight the goon from the other team, who is usually an alternate fourth-line forward or a bench-warming defenceman. I usually win; Dad taught me a few things about fighting over the years, whether he meant to or not.

You know that Johnny Cash song, the one where he says he had to get tough or die? Sometimes Wheelie Koontz plays that one when a penalty is called for fighting, and I feel like Johnny Cash is talking right to me as I skate over to the Sin Bin to spend five minutes (or less if the other team scores on the resulting power play, which they usually do).

I'm not just a goon, though. I hate being called that. I'll beat the shit out of you if you call me a goon. (That was a joke.) Considering the team I'm playing for, I'm actually a competent two-way defenceman, with a good plus-minus rating and a pretty hard shot from the point; I once scored from just inside the red line on Gasberg's starting goalie, who is already being scouted for the NHL.

My dad, on the other hand, *was* a goon. I'm not sure he ever scored a goal. If he did, nobody has ever mentioned it. They only ever talk about the fights.

My defence partner is Desi Desmond. Desi just barely made the team as a stay-at-home defenceman, but then again, pretty much all of us "just barely made the team." The talent pool is pretty shallow around here these days.

Desi is determined and unflappable, but he certainly isn't bursting with talent. While Keegan Thrush scores goals by impressively deking around opposing players with his nimble skating and skillful stickhandling, Desi gets the occasional point by taking hits in the corners and crashing the net. But mostly he blocks shots. He's got permanent welts all over his body to prove it. He's certainly prevented more goals against the Blue Flames this season than our goalie has.

Desi lives on East Derrick Street, the same as me. I'm on the west end, though, in one of the new rent-controlled buildings that the locals call "Cardboard Acres," while Desi lives on the east end, in one of the bow-roofed shacks near the railroad tracks. Yes, there is physically a "wrong side of the tracks" in Faireville.

The more well-to-do citizens of Faireville point to East Derrick whenever they want to scare their kids away from drugs and alcohol. Jokes are also made about inbreeding, especially at Desi's expense, since he isn't exactly a pretty-boy, with his tiny, close-set eyes; his wide, flat nose; and his crooked, yellow teeth.

Nobody in the arena is cheering for Desi Desmond. Or for me. Or for any other player on the roster for the Faireville Blue Flames. Not today.

And so it remains until now, the last minute of the final period of the game.

Keegan Thrush has already broken his own record for points scored by a single player in a Wheatfield League regular season hockey game, and somebody has probably already run across the street to the Faireville Pro Shop to get the trophy engraved.

Keegan scored three goals in the first seven minutes of the first period, and, to celebrate the hat trick, toques and baseball caps rained down on the ice like a primary-coloured hailstorm. It took the ref almost ten minutes to toss all of the headwear back over the glass.

Now we're in the last minute of the game, and Keegan's scored ten goals and added two assists; yes, a player on the Gasberg Pipefitters *not* named Keegan Thrush managed to get two pucks past our flustered goaltender at the beginning of the third period — goals that Keegan set up, of course, and only after he had scored ten himself.

The puck drops, and the game is on.

0:57

Keegan's already set a new league record for *points*, but still he presses forward. He wants to score that eleventh *goal.*

He skates through all of our defending forwards as if they're standing still, because compared to Keegan, they pretty much are. Keegan fires another hundred-mile-an-hour shot at our goaltender, but Desi Desmond leaps in front of it, blocking the shot with his chest.

0:49

My dad knows that he is not the most popular guy in town these days, and he usually tries to keep a low profile, but now he leaps to his feet and starts chanting, "Desi! Desi! Desi!" Desi Desmond's parents and sister, who are seated nearby, join the chant. But their small voices are drowned out by the roar of the mob, who respond by thundering, "KEEGAN! KEEGAN! KEEGAN!"

0:40

As the scoreboard clock continues counting down, Keegan picks up the rebound from Desi's chest and fires the puck at the top corner of the net, which he knows to be one of our goalie's (many) weak spots.

But a winded, panting Desi Desmond scrambles up onto his skates, leaps in the air, and punches at the flying puck with the knuckles of his battered glove, redirecting the puck just over the crossbar.

My dad jumps up and down, slapping his palms against the glass, screaming, "Desi! Desi! Desi!" But, against the volume of Keegan Thrush's fans, he might as well be mouthing the words.

"KEEGAN! KEEGAN! KEEGAN!"

0:33

Keegan flies around behind the net to regain possession of

the puck, but Desi meets him halfway and sends him flying with a perfectly placed hip check. Even over the frenzied roar that rattles the glass around the ice, you can hear the thump of their bodies colliding.

A few old timers who love physical hockey join in with Dad and Desi's family, barking, "Desi! Desi! Desi!" You can hear their voices now, faintly through the din.

Ramsay Thrush is watching the game from behind the glass where the Zamboni enters and exits the rink, away from the rest of the crowd. Am I imagining things, or did I just see the ref glance over at him and nod slightly?

The ref blows the whistle, and the clock stops.

0:22

"Penalty!" the ref cries. "Number twenty-seven, Desmond, two minutes for roughing!"

"Are you fucking KIDDING me?" my father shrieks. "Pretty Boy had the puck! That was a totally legal check!"

A few of the old timers nod along with my dad's assessment, but as Desi limps across the ice to the penalty box, shaking his head at the injustice of it all, the rest of the masses scream in delight. Their hero's team is about to get a power play! Keegan's eleventh goal is virtually guaranteed.

"KEEGAN! KEEGAN! KEEGAN!"

Keegan Thrush skates over to take the faceoff. He glances up at the clock: twenty-two seconds. The ref drops the puck, and Keegan wins the faceoff. He immediately takes his stick in both hands and slams our player in the chest, knocking him down to get him out of the way.

0:18

As our player falls to the ice, clutching his chest, gasping for breath, the arena continues to thunder with the mantra of the masses: "KEEGAN! KEEGAN! KEEGAN!"

My dad's protest cuts through the roar like a slender blade. "No call? NO FREAKIN' CALL? That's CROSS-CHECKING! Come ON!"

0:11

Keegan stickhandles through the three Blue Flames players jittering back and forth between him and the net.

0:08

He winds up and fires.

I jab out my stick, deflect the puck wide.

With his cheetah-like speed, Keegan Thrush has chased down the puck before I've even regained balance on my skates. Before our goalie even has time to reposition himself, Keegan spins and fires again.

0:04

The puck flies too close for me to do anything else, so I leap at it headfirst to block or deflect it. It cracks against my helmet, flies straight up in the air.

Keegan Thrush swats at the airborne puck, and the heel of his stick connects. The puck spirals through the air, arcs downward behind our goalie's shoulder, and wobbles on the ice just behind the goal line.

The adrenalized masses go insane.

"KEEGAN! KEEGAN! KEEGAN!"

"HIGH-STICKING!" my dad screams. "DISALLOW THE GOAL! DISALLOW THE GOAL!"

I know one thing with absolute certainty: the ref will not disallow that goal.

0:00

As the buzzer sounds to end the game, Keegan Thrush swings his stick in the air like a battleaxe and chops me in the back, right between the shoulder blades.

The cheering continues.

"KEEGAN! KEEGAN! KEEGAN!"

I'm on my knees on the ice. I try to catch my breath. I try to shake off the ringing in my ears. I try to will my vision to clear.

I've got to get up and make him pay for that. It's the Code.

My dad is trying to climb the glass to get at Keegan himself, but a bunch of other burly men are tugging him back down again. "DIRTY LITTLE FUCKER!" Dad hollers at Keegan. "DIRTY LITTLE FUCKER!"

"Come on, Pauly!" someone admonishes my dad. "Watch your language! There's kids here!"

By the time I'm able to rise up on my wobbly legs, Keegan Thrush is surrounded by the rest of the Gasberg Pipefitters, who are hugging and high-fiving him. The ref is over there, too, waiting for his turn to bestow accolades on the hero of the day.

Keegan's admiring teammates usher him toward their dressing room door, where Ramsay Thrush probably has chilled champagne and caviar waiting for them.

I'll never get to him now.

I'll never get to him, ever.

He will never have to pay.

I'm the last player to leave the ice.

I glance over at the glass where the Zamboni comes in and out. Keegan's dad is no longer there. He's probably gone out to his Maserati to write a cheque for the ref. It's probably not the first time he's done that.

My dad is gone, too. He's probably been escorted from the building by the Faireville Town Police. It isn't the first time for that, either. Dad knows all of the town cops by their first names.

My dad will probably try to start a fight with Keegan's dad in the arena parking lot. Dad will want to knee Ramsay Thrush in the balls, punch him in the stomach, slam his face against the trunk of his Maserati, over and over again, until the car's gleaming royal blue paint is stained purple from fresh red blood.

If not the police, then some stalwart citizens of Faireville will prevent this from happening; Ramsay Thrush is an upstanding civic leader and an admirable philanthropist. Pauly "The Pummeler" Springthorpe is a drunken has-been and an unemployed loser.

Keegan's dad will get to drive his record-breaking superstar son home in his Maserati, while my dad will probably be driven to a holding cell in the back of a police cruiser. It's all pretty much inevitable.

Up in the DJ booth, Wheelie Koontz is playing a song with the lyrics, "The winner takes it all, the loser takes the fall." Or something like that.

I sigh and skate toward the dressing room door.

I pull off my gloves and tuck them under my arm, then I pinch my "lucky" ring, and I twist it and twist it until it finally pulls free, taking bits of skin and blood with it. I drop the ring into the snow that's collected between the boards and the ice surface.

Maybe it will wind up inside the Zamboni. Maybe it will wind up embedded in the ice.

I don't care, I tell myself. *I'm finished with this game.*

But somewhere between the dressing room and the arena parking lot, I realize that none of this is the game's fault.

YYZ

Despite his battered, disconnected state, there is some jump in James Yeo's step. He strides along as his mental soundtrack plays "YYZ," the driving, guitar-bass-and-drums instrumental by Toronto rock band Rush.

YYZ is the identification code for Toronto's Pearson International Airport. It's the Morse code signal that guides the planes in, and these three letters are printed on the luggage tags of anyone returning to Toronto after escaping to anywhere else by air. If James hadn't *consciously* chosen the song, his subconscious would have played the track anyway.

At this late hour of the night (or, depending on one's perspective, this early hour of the morning) no planes land at Terminal One. Except for the whir of ventilation fans and the hum of idling computers and muted TV screens, the fluorescent-lit expanse of YYZ is silent. Other than the occasional security officer or cleaner who ambles past, the usually-bustling space is inert and lifeless.

James stands and stares up into the antiseptically clean, heaven-bright expanse of Terminal One — the curved panes of glass, the triangulated white cantilevers — and he feels a slight tingle of hope from somewhere within his heart's compressed tangle of flaps and tissues and arteries. He can feel his blood pumping inside him; James Yeo knows that he is still alive.

James reaches into his briefcase and tugs the laptop computer out. He flips it open, switches it on, and clicks "YES" to connect to the airport's wireless Internet. First he logs on to the Riskey and Gamble corporate website and navigates to the customer service blog that he is required to update once a day. He types:

James Yeo is going away.

Next, James signs in to his LinkedIn page, another Web presence required of all sales staff at Riskey and Gamble. "Gotta keep your clients informed!" Harry says. So, James informs his clients:

James Yeo is going away.

Then onto his Facebook page. In the status bar he types:

James Yeo is going away.

And then onto Twitter, where he Tweets:

James Yeo is going away.

And then he sets his Gmail account to respond to incoming emails with the following automatic response:

James Yeo is going away.

A hot wave washes over his cool brain, and his eyelids flutter. His head lolls back against the back of the blue-on-chrome chair. On James's mental soundtrack, "YYZ" is still playing, but the tempo slows and the volume gradually drops.

The bright, white expanse of Pearson International Airport fades to a foggy shade of grey, and then into a void of black, through which the eye of James Yeo's mind floats back to the previous morning, which already seems like a lifetime ago.

Declination

dec-lin-a-tion

dɛk ləˈneɪ ʃən

1. A bending, sloping, or moving downward (as a spent rocket falling to Earth).
2. Deterioration.
3. Deviation, as from a standard.

MOVING IS EASIER THAN RENOVATING

James Yeo strokes the strings one last time, and as that final melancholy minor chord echoes back at him from the concrete walls of the Air Canada Centre, the capacity crowd roars its approval.

Leaning against the security barrier in the front row of the crowd is Priya; she waves her hands in the air, and her .22-calibre nipples strain against her Rush *Moving Pictures* concert jersey. James winks at her, and she smiles.

"Thank you, Toronto!" he says into the microphone, his equalized voice amplified to demigod volume. "It's good to be home."

Then the bedside clock radio blares; the crowd vanishes, the mic disappears, and James no longer feels the guitar strap digging into his right shoulder.

He jolts upright in bed, once again failing to recognize the interior of their most recent bedroom. James and Sidney have switched houses five times in the past three years, and sometimes his waking mind still expects to surface somewhere else.

James's wife, Sidney, is a real estate agent, and she had felt that it was "imperative" to sell their previous home while the market was "hot," and to upgrade to a place with Premium Selling Features while mortgage rates were low. So they flipped their solid little double-brick wartime home in "scorching white-hot Leaside" and exchanged it for a seven-digit mortgage and an enormous, stucco-and-fibreboard suburban McMansion near Avenue and Wilson.

Their latest residence is way up north by Highway 401, at the opposite end of the city from where they both work, a frustrating crosstown journey from where any of their friends live, a war zone of snarled traffic and construction zones and closed roads and one-way streets between their house and any point within the city where they might actually want or need to be. Despite these "minor lifestyle accommodations," though, Sidney is pleased; they now possess a house with the following Premium Selling Features:

- A three-car garage! (For their single Honda Civic, which Sidney is suddenly itching to replace with a Lexus sedan.)
- Twelve-foot ceilings! (A twelve-rung ladder is necessary to change the "contractor-grade" pot lights, one of which seems to burn out weekly.)
- A kitchen cooktop with six burners! (They have used two of them so far: one to boil pasta, the other to warm the sauce-from-a-jar.)
- A family room, a living room, *and* a rec room! (James and Sidney currently own enough furniture to partially furnish the rec room.)
- Four big bedrooms! (Three of which have not yet been slept in.)
- A heated driveway! ("Nice!" James mused. "We can switch it on in the winter to give the local homeless people something warm sleep on." Sidney rolled her eyes and huffed, "It's for melting *snow*, James. There are no *homeless people* in *this* neighbourhood.")

The biggest Premium Selling Feature of them all, though, in Sidney's Professional Opinion? *Seven* bathrooms! *SEVEN!* Her voice trembled with emotion as they signed the mortgage documents. "We will make a *killing* when we flip *this* place!"

James understands now that no house they share can ever really be a home; in Sid's own words, it's merely a "deficit-financed equity upgrade." He hasn't bothered unpacking all his clothes from the suitcases yet, and his guitars are still sealed inside cardboard travelling closets rented from the moving company, whose drivers know James and Sidney by their first names. James is wary of letting himself get too comfortable here, since Sidney and her colleagues are already predicting that their new neighbourhood is going to get "very hot, very soon."

If James complains even obliquely about the hassle of moving homes approximately every eight months, Sidney just shrugs and says, "Moving is easier than renovating." Or, alternately: "I deserve better. I deserve more." There is a hardcover book on Sidney's bedside table that reminds her daily of her newfound mantra:

YOU DESERVE BETTER!
YOU DESERVE MORE!
Rule the Boardroom! Rule the Bedroom! Rule the World!

James notes cynically that reading this book has not resulted in more bedroom proclivity from his wife; in fact, their sexual liaisons have actually *decreased* since she started reading this tome.

"... and it's going to be the hottest day of the season so far," an over-caffeinated DJ hollers through the speaker of the clock radio, "a record-breaking thirty degrees Celsius, or eighty-six degrees Fahrenheit. So get out there and make the most of a —"

"Oh, shuddup!" Sidney moans as she pounds the snooze button with her fist, glaring at the LED digits glowing *6:00 a.m.* "Gawwwwwd! Why is it so fucking hot in here?"

"I can go switch on the air conditioning if you want."

James is not sure he can actually do this, since the state-of-the-art, multi-zone forced-air system has a control grid more elaborate than the instrument panel of a Boeing 747.

"Gawd," Sidney whines, "this humidity is insufferable!"

She kicks her long, slim legs in the air, launching the Egyptian-cotton sheets and Indian silk–covered duvet off herself, and burying James beneath them. The hem of her nightdress lands eight inches above her smooth pubic mound, which she recently had waxed bald at the spa; the little bloody speckles have just faded away.

James was fond of Sidney's sparse triangle of strawberry-blond pubic hair, and he wonders why she would so abruptly remove a feature of her body that he had praised so frequently. Nevertheless, the sight of his wife lying there with her legs wide open, pubic hair or none, causes James's erection to push up hard against the heap of down-filled bedding.

He shrugs the duvet and sheets onto the floor and then rolls over toward Sidney, brushing the inside of her thigh with his fingertips. A few gentle stokes there used to be all it took to get her juices flowing. Just a few months ago, she would have been on top of him right away.

She snaps her legs together, trapping his hand.

"For gawd's sake, James!"

"Aw, c'mon, Sid."

She tugs his fingers out, pulls down the nightdress, and props herself up against her custom-made, virgin-down-filled Medium-Firm Side-Sleeper pillow. The muscles of Sidney's trainer-toned arms are lean, tense, and twitchy.

"No time for *that*," she says. "I've got to show three different houses this morning, and I still have to wash and straighten my hair. This fucking humidity!"

James reaches for her waist and says, "Just let it go curly today."

"Professional women *do not* have curly hair," she says.

Apparently, James muses, *neither above nor below*.

"And you'd better get your ass in gear, too," Sidney says. She swings her legs over the side of the bed, and her feet slap against the polished rainforest-hardwood floor before James can touch her again. "You can't slack off just because you're married to the boss's daughter."

James sighs. As if working for Sidney's father has ever been an advantage.

Sid's dear daddy had invited more guests to their wedding than James had. Harry Riskey's VIP clients and colleagues sat closer to the head table than James's own mother and father. After the wedding, Sidney's parents sent around little albums of photos from the event to all of the guests, embossed in gold leaf with *Our Daughter Sidney's Wedding* (as opposed to, say, *James and Sidney's Wedding*). Harry Riskey vetoed the photo of James removing the garter belt in the traditional fashion, from beneath his daughter's wedding dress, judging it to be "inappropriate to share with colleagues and clients"; but somehow another photo, which depicted Harry's business partner, Baldric Gamble, posing beside the non-blushing bride, her left buttock clenched firmly in his right hand, slipped through the approval process.

The photo album pretty much summed it up for James; he, the groom, in his tuxedo with the dusty-rose-pink bow tie and vest, was of equivalent value to the proceedings as the dusty-rose-pink bridesmaids' dresses and the dusty-rose-pink ribbons tied around the chair backs at the reception.

During the Pregnancy Scare, Harry Riskey had made three demands:

1. James would immediately cut his long hair short.
2. James would immediately quit playing music for a living and would come to work at Riskey and Gamble Insurance.
3. James would marry Sidney within three months, before Sidney's pregnancy started to show in an obvious way.

Even after it was discovered that the pregnancy test had showed a false positive, James complied with all three of Harry Riskey's demands.

And here James is now.

"And don't leave that bedding on the floor!" Sidney scolds. "Those sheets are dry clean only, and that duvet cover cost three thousand dollars!"

James picks up the sheets and duvet, and smoothes them over the mattress.

James follows Sidney into the ensuite.

She leans over the faux-marble countertop, her face an inch from the bevelled mirror as she inserts her contact lenses. "By the way, you'll have to eat dinner by yourself tonight, okay?"

James inches up behind her and encircles her waist in his hands. "Showing houses tonight, too?" he asks.

His erection springs free from his boxer shorts, and he nestles it between her upturned cheeks.

"Oh, for gawd's sake, James, stop that. It isn't romantic."

"But it's fun!"

"Maybe for you."

"I can't help it! You have the nicest ass!"

"Well, you're right about that," she says. "And no, I'm not showing houses tonight. I'm having a strategy meeting with Roland."

James's penis deflates, and he steps back from his wife's previously enticing buttocks.

Roland. Roland Baron. Roland "The Red" Baron. The self-proclaimed "Baron of the Upper Beach." That's what it says on his business cards, embossed in faux-gold letters right beneath his grinning mug shot, along with the phrase *You Deserve Better! You Deserve More!* Since it was Roland Baron who gave the book to Sidney, James assumes that the business card slogan was plagiarized directly from the book's cover.

James has five of Roland's cards, one for each time that Roland has forgotten (or pretended to forget) that they've met before.

"Nice to meet you, Jake," Roland says (every time), handing over his card as if it's the key to the city.

"We've met before," James replies (every time). "And it's James."

James can't even purge any of his passive-aggressive anger by drawing a ridiculous goatee over Roland's business card photo, because Roland already has one, trimmed so immaculately that it appears to be etched onto his chin with a black Magic Marker.

For the past three business quarters, Roland Baron has been the Top Grossing Agent at the real estate brokerage where Sidney works; he's got the translucent plastic tombstones on his desk to prove it. Roland claims that he invented the term "the Upper Beach," and now he is the dominant real estate agent in the area.

The Beach itself is a neighbourhood that runs parallel to the eastern beaches along Lake Ontario. For the sort of Torontonians who have become rich from capitalism but still want to feel as cool as they did during their wannabe-hippie-underground-university-newspaper days, this "upscale yet funky" area is *the* place to own a home. Some of the old-timers still call it *the Beaches*, but the influx of Limousine Liberals voted to rename it *the Beach*. Simple. Elegant. Refined. Like the people who have taken over the area. And yes, they actually had a *referendum* on the issue. It was *that* important.

Just to the north of the Beach is the southwest corner of Scarborough, a satellite of Toronto that is a bit too low-rent and working-class for the bankers and lawyers from the downtown office towers. Coffee Time franchises still outnumber Starbucks, and there is more Bud Light on tap than any imported or micro-brewery beer, so properties in Scarborough are a harder sell to the nouveaux riches.

Then Roland Baron had an idea, a great, Grinchy idea: instead of "Southwest Scarborough," he would refer to the area as "the Upper Beach," and maybe some reluctant neo-capitalists would pay premium prices to live there. As Roland explains it, "When you meet some chick from Mississauga at a downtown night-club, and she asks you where you live, *the Upper Beach* sounds pretty cool, right? I mean, Mississauga is *Manhattan* compared to Scarborough, but you just might get into that tight little, um, *minidress* of hers" — he winks here — "if you live in *the Upper Beach*. Am I right, or am I right? Or am I right?"

By the time the other real estate agents had caught on to the ploy, Roland was already the Baron of the Upper Beach, with his name and likeness plastered onto giant billboards all over the area. Since he now had more business than one agent could possibly handle by himself, he benevolently offered a "limited partnership" to his colleague Sidney.

Their partnership doesn't have many limits, as far as James can tell.

Since "joining forces" with Roland, Sidney wears low-cut blouses and push-up bras, because one of Roland's maxims is "Mammaries Move Properties." She wears thong-style panties now, too, because, according to the Baron of the Upper Beach, "Panty Lines Discourage Signings." Or maybe the saying was "Ass Sells Grass."

Sidney has replaced their coffee maker, which James's grandparents gave them as a wedding gift, with an espresso machine just like Roland's, brought in from Italy by some importer with whom Roland attended prep school. Sidney also wants to trade in their perfectly good Honda Civic for a Lexus sedan like Roland drives. In the words of Roland Baron, "Your Car Is What You Are." Or, in Sid's own words, "You can keep driving that shitty old Honda if you want to, James; I deserve better. I deserve more."

"That's what the Red Buffoon's card says," James observed.

"Don't call him that," Sidney snapped. "Your jealousy of Roland is so … palpable. It's not attractive, James."

Sidney has also been shopping around for a bigger diamond for the engagement ring that James bought her, even though the original cost him more than he spent on his first three cars, including their current Honda Civic. Roland says, "Winners Wear Their Winnings," and apparently nothing says *Winner* more than a huge chunk of polymorphous carbon on one's finger.

Sidney deserves better. Sidney deserves more. Roland Baron has told her so.

The Red Buffoon sends text messages to James's wife almost hourly, and Sidney always responds immediately, even during their third-anniversary dinner last month. Just last night, Sidney's omnipresent smartphone buzzed at 1:45 a.m.; it was Roland, sending her pictures of the precious dessert he was eating at some precious downtown restaurant with a six-month waiting list and no prices on the menu.

"Does he have any idea what time it is?" James grumbled.

"Winners Get Up Early, and They Go to Bed Late," Sidney said.

"Why the hell is he sending you photos of his chocolate soufflé?"

"It's decorated with *edible gold leaf*," Sidney said. "He's actually eating *twenty-four carat gold*!"

"His morning bowel movement will be quite a commodity."

"Just go back to sleep," Sidney sighed, as her spa-manicured nails continued clickity-clacking on the keypad of her phone.

James turns away from the mirror in the ensuite and tucks his mostly flaccid unit back into his boxers.

"Didn't you just have a 'strategy meeting' with Roland last week?"

"Business is booming," Sidney says. She stares into her own eyes in the mirror as she eliminates a single, imperfect eyebrow hair with zircon-encrusted tweezers. "We've got a lot to discuss."

"I can cook something when you get home," James says. "I don't mind waiting for you."

"This was our best sales month since we joined forces," Sidney says, "so Roland is taking me to Canoe to celebrate."

Ah. *Canoe.* One of those restaurants where nobody pays the bill with their own money. If you don't have a corporate expense account, or if you aren't deducting the cost to reduce your net income on your tax return, you probably aren't dining at Canoe.

"Oh, okay then," says James. "Well, I've got a doctor's appointment this afternoon at Yonge and Eglinton, so maybe I could meet you and Roland at Canoe! Maybe he'll remember my name this time."

"No, James. This is a business meeting. Absolutely not." Her voice echoes inside the hollow of the faux-Moroccan-mosaic-tiled shower enclosure. "And if you want people to remember your name, then, well ... be more memorable."

"Maybe I should punch that smug motherfucker right on his shoe-polish goatee. I bet he'd find that *memorable*."

"Don't be a Neanderthal, James," she says, turning her back to him. Then, over her shoulder, "Oh, I almost forgot. Priya wants you to stop by and help her hang some mirrors or something."

Priya is Sidney's former college roommate, to whom she sometimes lends James as a "rental husband."

"Oh," James says. "Okay. So, you have fun with the Red Buffoon, and I'll have fun with Priya."

But Sidney doesn't hear him. She doesn't even seem to see him anymore. She's pulled the tinted-glass shower door closed, and the hot water hisses from seven separate jets (another Premium Selling Feature). The water blasts her skin, dripping from her strawberry nipples, cascading over her lean, muscular shoulders and back. Rivulets cling to her tight, flat belly, twist around her long, lean legs. Vine-like streams flow over her round, personal-trainer-sculpted behind.

Tonight she'll wriggle into that shimmering top that clings to her breasts like wet, black spray paint. She'll pull on that skirt that stops halfway down her thighs, the one that tucks in under her ass just right, and those dark nylons he loves, the ones with the lines up the back. And that thong James gave her for Valentine's Day, that awesome pink one that folds just slightly into the now-hairless crease between her legs; *that* will get him going for sure.

Sidney runs her slippery hands over the hard, tight contours of her body. *Premium Selling Features indeed,* she thinks.

James wanders into the only other bathroom that ever gets used, and once his own shower is running from its single spout, he allows himself to fantasize about Priya.

They are painting the hallway in her apartment; he does the rolling, Priya does the details. Her breasts rise and her soft buttocks lift as she reaches with her paintbrush to touch up a spot she missed near the ceiling.

Her long, straight black hair still falls in her face when she blushes or smiles, and that tinge in her deep brown eyes of … of what? What is it? Longing? Wisdom? Sadness? Regret? Whatever it is, that subtle tone somehow changes her from merely pretty to a rare kind of beautiful. And that aspect of her, whatever it is, never fails to arouse James. It makes him want to taste her, to touch her, to thrill her, to fill her with pleasure.

Priya catches him admiring her and smiles.

"Do you want to take a break with me, James?" she says. She peels off her paint-speckled yoga pants and brushes past him in the narrow hallway. He follows her into the small living room, where she lies back on her ancient sofa and opens up for him, her thatch of jet-black fur trimmed neatly around the edges, just the way James likes it.

James begins stroking himself, feeling as if the rushing water is the only thing preventing him from bursting into flames and crumbling into a pillar of ash.

INCONVENIENCE

When the argument begins, I'm trapped inside the "Employees Only" washroom at the back of the Gas 'n' Snak convenience store. I'm not an actual employee of the Gas 'n' Snak, but because my wheelchair won't fit inside the washroom that's reserved for customers, Khalid lets me use this one instead.

"I'm sorry, sir," Khalid's voice says, "but until you comply with my request, I'm afraid that I cannot serve you."

"Look," the other voice says, "just gimme my smokes, my lottery tickets, and my burritos, and we're done here. Mmm-kay, Gandhi?"

Their voices are getting louder out there, but right now I can't do anything to help Khalid.

Khalid is my best friend. When my mom is working the night shift at the hospital, she drops me off here to keep Khalid company. Or for Khalid to keep me company, whichever. She doesn't have to worry about me when I'm hanging out here at the Gas 'n' Snak. There isn't much trouble I can get into here, she figures. Still, between the sporadic bursts of customers buying premium gasoline for their cars and two-for-one microwaved burritos for their children, Khalid and I manage to keep ourselves entertained:

- We drink "complimentary" cherry cola Slushees. Khalid says it's okay to have a free one now and then, since there's really no way to track how much of the syrupy guck is actually consumed by humans and how much gets spilled and drained away into the sewers, probably creating hyperactive, high-fructose-corn-syrup-mutated frogs and catfish down there in that fertile water.
- We peruse the restricted magazines with titles like *Penthouse Letters, Juggs, Biker Mamas,* and *MILF International* from the top shelf of the rack. We find most of the content hilarious rather than titillating. "Hey, look at Bunny McBoobs, who is washing a sports car with her ridiculous artificial breasts!" or "Miss Sex Ed Teacher is going to teach those thirty-year-old 'boys' in her classroom a thing or two about discipline!"
- We laugh at the customers who scramble back to their cars with the magazines they've purchased from the top shelf. It's usually older men; I guess they've never used the Internet for anything but email and the Weather Network. It tends to be guys who wear glasses and/or cardigan sweaters who buy *Penthouse Letters*, while *Juggs* seems to be the favourite of guys who've got, um, "juggs" themselves. *Biker Mamas* generally go home with Biker Papas, and *MILF International* is favoured by guys around our own age, guys whose moms must be regulating their Internet usage, guys who are probably really into our English teacher, Ms. Womansfield (who changed her name from "Mansfield" after her divorce).

- We talk about whatever happened at school that day, which usually takes about five minutes. If you're not on the football team, or a cheerleader, or in the school band, or in the photography or yearbook or Bible Study clubs, not much happens at Faireville District High School, except for when the occasional kid falls asleep at his desk and then gets laughed at by the other kids.

Nobody at school calls Khalid by his actual name; when he and his mom immigrated to our little town a few years ago, he was immediately nicknamed "the Sheik." Nobody was being nasty, or racist, or anything like that, though. Faireville is made up of ninety-nine percent white people, so Khalid seemed kind of exotic to them, I guess. When one of the girls noticed that Khalid looks sort of like that old black-and-white movie star Rudolph Valentino, who was nicknamed "the Sheik," well, the name just kind of stuck, I guess.

Khalid doesn't mind the nickname, anyway. He says that in Pakistan, the term "sheikh" is used to signify Arab descent and is reserved for people with great wealth and status. Khalid isn't Arab, and if he had any money or power he wouldn't be working at the Gas 'n' Snak every night after school to help his mom pay the rent on their one-bedroom apartment. So, I suppose the nickname is really kind of a compliment, right?

"The Sheik" is better than anyone else's nickname, anyway. The kids at Faireville District High School aren't very imaginative. They call Jimmy Rogers "Zig-Zag," because that's the brand of papers he uses to roll his joints. They call Marty Apostrophes "Farty Marty," not because Marty is any more or less flatulent than anyone else, but simply because "Farty" rhymes with "Marty," I suppose.

My own nickname is "Wheelie." Because I'm in a wheelchair. Ha ha! Get it? Pretty creative, huh?

At the moment, my wheelchair is being a bigger pain in the butt than usual. Somebody is out there hollering at my best friend, and there is nothing I can do to help him, because my rear wheel is jammed underneath the washroom's sink. Again.

"I'm sorry, sir," Khalid says, "but this is the third time this week that you have parked in the spot reserved for people with disabilities. I will not serve you until you move your car to another space."

"Look," the other voice says, "don't play the 'poor handicapped people' card on me, okay? It isn't fair that the best spot in the lot is reserved for the retards. Most of 'em can't drive, anyway, and I guarantee you, I pay more taxes than any of them do. So just gimme my smokes, my lottery tickets, and my burritos, and I'll move my car to my nice, heated garage at home. Mmm-kay, Gandhi?"

Khalid persists, ignoring the Gandhi comment. "As soon as you move your car to an appropriate parking spot, we can complete your transaction."

"What the hell difference does it make?" the other voice moans. "I don't see any handicapped people around, do you?"

This would be an ideal moment for me to burst out of the back room and roll out into the fluorescent light.

I rock my chair back and forth to get myself unstuck, but this just lodges the wheel in even deeper. If somebody at Gas 'n' Snak corporate headquarters had issued a directive requiring wheelchair-accessible washrooms in all of their stores, I would already be out there helping their employee, my friend.

I stretch my arms as far as they'll go, hyperextending my joints to reach the liquid soap dispenser that is nailed loosely to the wall. I'll use some soap to lubricate my jammed wheel and get myself unstuck.

I grip both rear wheels in my hands, and I wrench them back and forth as hard as I can, until the soap-lubricated tire finally springs free from underneath the sink.

I ram my chair's footrests against the door, over and over again, until it springs open with a dramatic crack.

I wheel myself out into the fluorescent glare of the store, where Khalid is standing face to face with a barrel-bellied man in a business suit, with only the cash counter between them.

They don't notice my dramatic entrance, though, because I'm mostly hidden behind a tall cardboard display for spicy beef jerky.

Khalid leans forward on the counter, his lean biceps and triceps twitching beneath his shining brown skin, his wiry frame towering over his opponent, and he says, "I'm not serving you until you move your car to another spot, *sir*." He spits out a particularly sarcastic "sir."

"You've seen my car, right?" the Suit Man says. "It's a fucking *Maserati.* If I park in one of the regular narrow parking spots, some yahoo in a shitty old truck will swing his door open and dent my car."

Looking very much like a sheik, Khalid stares coolly at his nemesis.

"The *yahoos* in this town, as you so eloquently put it, have the decency to refrain from parking in the handicapped spot."

I glance out into the parking lot, and my eyes narrow. This suit-wearing, Maserati-driving, *ambulatory* jerk is indeed parked on top of the blue-and-white symbol of a wheelchair, the spot reserved for people with physical disabilities; the spot reserved for *me*.

My pulse begins to throb in my neck. I wheel myself around the beef jerky display, and I clear my throat loudly

When he sees me, Mr. Maserati stammers, "Oh, well, okay, I see. I didn't know there was one in here."

And then, as if he is speaking to a toddler, as if I've got a mental handicap to go with my spina bifida, he crouches down and says to me, in this singsong kindergarten teacher's voice, "I'll move my car when your bus shows up, okay, buddy? Attaboy."

Attaboy. As if I'm a *puppy.*

I tell him, "You need to move your fucking car."

"Whoa, buddy!" Mr. Maserati says. "You got Tourette's or something?"

I repeat, "Move your fucking car."

"I'll only be a minute," he says, in that same pitchy voice. "Sorry about the inconvenience, buddy."

Sometimes it *is* inconvenient when the parking spot isn't available; in the winter, wheeling my way to the Gas 'n' Snak through the ice and slush is a tough slog, and the spokes of my wheels toss mucky water up all over my legs, and the wheel brakes get crusted with ice and won't work properly. It's not the inconvenience that bothers me so much, though. It's the disrespect.

I tell Mr. Maserati, "Being unable to walk is more than an *inconvenience.*"

"Hey, buddy, I understand," he says, in that same patronizing tone of voice. "It's tough. I get it. I had my leg in a cast for a month after a football injury, so I get it. I *sympathize.* Mmm-kay, buddy? Attaboy."

He makes a move like he is going to pat me on the head. I swing a fist at him.

"Whoa!" he chuckles, stepping easily out of the radius of my punch. "You're a feisty one!"

Then he waves a dismissive hand at me and turns back to Khalid. "So, what's it gonna be, Gandhi? I'm not moving until you give me my stuff. I can stand here all night if I have to."

Khalid folds his arms across his chest. "So can I."

"You're not gonna win this, kid."

"It is you who is not going to win this, *sir.*"

"Do you know who I am?" Mr. Maserati says.

"Do you know who *I* am?" the Sheik counters.

It looks like this standoff is going to last for a while.

I wheel myself back through the stockroom of the Gas 'n' Snak, past the now-broken "Employees Only" washroom door, to the utility closet where they keep the tools. It's a bit of a stretch from down here, but I manage to reach up high and pull free a narrow-tipped screwdriver from its clip on the tool board. This ought to do the trick.

I push my chair through the steel-plated "Deliveries Only" entrance and out into the parking lot. The narrow tires of my wheelchair hum against the asphalt as I speed toward the gleaming, midnight-blue Maserati. It *is* a beautiful car; too bad it's owned by such an asshole.

I reach down and twist off the black rubber cap from the valve on the Maserati's front passenger-side tire. There is a satisfying *HISSSSSSSSSSSSSS* as I jam the tip of the screwdriver into the valve. It doesn't take long for the low-profile, rubber band tire to deflate.

I wheel backward and give the rear tire the same treatment, then I roll around to the back of the car; I'm contemplating carving the word *asshole* into the gleaming paint above the licence plate frame that reads "Gasberg Exotic Sports Cars," when Mr. Maserati barrels out from the Gas 'n' Snak, his belly wobbling as he runs. A plastic Gas 'n' Snak bag dangles from his right fist.

"Hey! Hey! Hey!" Khalid screams, sprinting after him. "You can't leave without paying! Get back here!"

"Take it out of your pay, Gandhi!" Mr. Maserati cackles. "And don't start fights with winners, loser!"

My tires squawk on the pavement as I race away from the Maserati as fast as my burning arms will move me. I almost dump my chair over as I turn the sharp corner to hide behind the Dumpster. I hear the car door slamming, the roar of the Maserati's engine revving, the shriek of tires, Khalid's voice hollering, "I've got you on video! I've got you on video!"

I peek around the corner of the Dumpster, just in time to see the speeding Maserati cut a corner too sharply; its door screeches against the side of a telephone pole.

"Attaboy," I grumble.

Perhaps the driver oversteered because his tires were under-inflated. Too bad. Such a beautiful car.

Sorry about the inconvenience, buddy.

PROPERTY OF RISKEY AND GAMBLE

From inside his cramped, putty-grey office cubicle, James Yeo is cold-calling a potential new client.

"No, Sheila — may I call you Sheila? — this isn't a joke," he says, repeating the target's name over and over again to create a false sense of intimacy, as he has been trained to do. "Yes, Sheila, the name of our brokerage really is Riskey and Gamble Insurance."

The company, of course, is named after James's father-in-law, Harrison Riskey, and Baldric Gamble, Riskey's best friend since their business school fraternity days. Among the expense-account raconteurs at their old boys' club, they are known as Harry and Baldy, and much fun is made of the fact that Baldy sports a thick mane of silver-grey hair, while Harry's dome is as smooth and polished as an infant's baby-oiled bottom. As a pair, their "street names" remind James of the kinda gangsta boyz who'd mess ya up real bad fer missin' a payment, but their five-thousand-dollar suits, hundred-thousand-dollar cars, and multi-million dollar homes put them in the exclusive category of privileged men who can afford to have others throw the punches for them.

"I assure you, Sheila," James continues, reading from the script on the computer screen, "signing on with Riskey and Gamble is neither risky nor a gamble. However, insuring with our competition could be either, or both. Our company slogan is, and always has been, 'Riskey and Gamble: Safe and Sound.'"

The slogan reminds James of Big Brother's Doublespeak in George Orwell's *1984*: *"War Is Peace," "Freedom Is Slavery," "Ignorance Is Strength," "Risky Is Safe," "A Gamble Is Sound."* He has never shared this observation with Harry or Baldy, though.

Once, when James joked that the cold calls would be a lot easier if they had just named the company Safe and Sound Insurance in the first place, Harry Riskey raged that "Real men put their real names on their accomplishments! That's what real men do, Jimmy! Real men don't hide behind fake names!"

Harry and Baldy roared with laughter, knowing that James used to play guitar and sing his original songs in pubs under the stage name James Why. (Incidentally, since coming to work at Riskey and Gamble, James has not performed live once. He has not written a single new song. He hardly even sings in the shower anymore.)

Harry and Baldy speed-walk through the office, neither interacting with any of their inferiors. Both men would rather be out on a members-only golf course or at the club drinking premium Scotch with other men in five-thousand-dollar suits. When they actually show up at their twenty-seventh-floor business, they prefer the sunlit, polished-wood panelling of their adjacent corner offices to the fluorescent glare and putty-grey of their minions' cubicles. Also, Harry and Baldy's offices have well-stocked mini-bars, while the proles make do with a coin-operated coffee machine (currently out of order).

As Harry Riskey passes James's cubicle, he grunts, "Gawddammit, Jimmy, I'm not paying you to daydream."

James hates it when Harry calls him "Jimmy." It makes him feel like some subservient pup, nipping hopefully at the Big Boss's heels (which is exactly how Harry Riskey *wants* his son-in-law to feel). It is never wise to correct Harry, though, so James once again allows himself to be called "Jimmy."

"Well, actually," James says, "I just got off a call with a client who agreed to —"

"Then get on *another* call!" Riskey barks. "Selling insurance policies pays the bills around here, and your salary is one of the bills. So sell some more gawd-damned insurance policies, Jimmy!"

James assumes that Harry's aggression is just alpha-male posturing meant to impress Baldy, but he still finds the bile difficult to swallow. Thanks to his friend Ranjeev in Accounting, James knows that he is the top salesperson in his division, yet he takes home the lowest salary. But he also knows better than to complain. Riskey and Gamble Insurance has a closed compensation system, meaning that nobody is allowed to know how much money anyone else makes. The theory is that removing wage competition between employees creates a more "trusting" work environment. This "trust" is well enforced, contractually: *Any employee of Riskey and Gamble can and will be terminated without severance for revealing their financial compensation to another employee.*

"Well, don't just sit there with your mouth open, Jimmy," Harry huffs over his shoulder as he struts away from James's cubicle, "get on another call, for Chrissakes! Winners win, and losers lose. You have to decide which one you're going to be, and be it. Have you even started reading the Book yet?"

Of course, "the Book" that Harry is referring to is:

YOU DESERVE BETTER!
YOU DESERVE MORE!
Rule the Boardroom! Rule the Bedroom! Rule the World!

Harry was overjoyed when he discovered that there was already a copy in James and Sidney's house; he and Baldy both have signed copies displayed prominently atop the desks in their respective corner offices.

James ignores the question about the Book, and says, "Actually, Harry, I'm just wrapping up my cold-calling docket, so I can —"

Harry stops in his tracks, and, without turning around, says, "Don't call me Harry when we're in the office, Jimmy."

"Um, sorry, Mr. Riskey," James rephrases, "but what I was trying to say earlier was that I'm wrapping up my calls for the day because I've got the afternoon off. I cleared it with Sanchez last week. If I don't leave right now, I'll be late for my appointment."

"You can reschedule your manicure for the weekend, Jimmy," Harry says.

From inside his office, Baldy guffaws and then breaks into one of his frequent coughing fits. His daily lunchtime cigar-and-cognac habit isn't doing his aging body any favours.

"Well, actually, Mr. Riskey," James says, "it's a *medical* appointment. Um, you know, a *follow-up* medical appointment."

Harry Riskey spins around, strides back over to James's cubicle. He towers over his son-in-law, raising his chin so that the point on his impeccably trimmed beard is aimed right between James's eyes, like an ancient king staring down an inept serf. Twice a week, Harry pays more than James earns in a day to have his grey facial hair groomed like the putting greens at his members-only club.

"Jimmy," he says in a stage whisper, "is this about your sperm count?"

"Um, possibly, sir," James says. "They, uh, wouldn't say over the phone."

"Well, for Chrissakes," Harry says, his eyes wide, "get yourself out of here! Go! Now!"

In the past two years, Harry Riskey has had three at-fault car accidents, two massive heart attacks, and one rectal polyp removal, all of which have caused him to suspect that he might not live forever. More than anything else in the world, Harry wants a rightful heir to his fortune and legacy, a young man whom he can sculpt after his own great likeness. And it has to be a young *man*; Harrison Riskey is a true believer in Patriarchal Lineage. His only legitimate offspring, Sidney, was supposed to be his heir apparent, but of course his wife got one of the chromosomes wrong, and Sidney came out female. So, at Harry's age, a grandson is really his only hope, and hence Harry's great interest in the well-being of James's sperm.

"I'll call my driver to take you to your appointment," Harry says.

"Okay," James says. "Thanks, Mr. Riskey."

"You can call me Harry when we're talking family business, Jimmy. The limo driver will be waiting in the foyer."

"Thanks, um, Harry," James says.

James and his sperm have never been invited to ride in the Riskey and Gamble company car before. There is a rare bounce in his step as he zigs and zags around the other putty-grey cubicles to escape for the day.

Just as the elevator doors slide open, Harry Riskey calls out to James, "Take your laptop with you. You can work on policy forms and answer client emails from the doctor's waiting room. This isn't a vacation, Jimmy."

James slinks back to his desk to pick up his company-issued laptop, which is embossed with the words *Property of Riskey and Gamble*.

MAPLE LEAF SERMON

Game Seven, Round Two of the playoffs. Just five bucks a seat to see the Leafs play the Devils on the Sony Jumbotron at the Air Canada Centre. Come one, come all!

Having paid just one-fiftieth the price of a regular-season live game ticket, the blue-and-white masses converge on The Hangar, from Oshawa, from Pickering, from Mississauga, from Scarborough, from Hamilton, from London, and from between and beyond. For many, it's the first time they've entered the temple; the season tickets are mostly owned by Bay Street business types, who don't even return to their seats from the bar until the middle of the second period.

But these are the Faithful, these are the True Fans. Oh, hear the pre-game thunder! Six thousand voices, voices usually confined to suburban basement rec rooms; the roar reaches out into the streets.

Outside the arena, a man with bone-thin arms and rawhide leather skin is shaking his dreadlocks and a makeshift Stanley Cup, which he has made from a dented public washroom garbage can and a tomato-juice tin crowned with a margarine container.

The man smells of stale sweat and dust and urine, and he is clothed in dirt-scrubbed robes, like a battle-worn Jesus (or maybe it's Mohammed, or perhaps these sheets were all he could scavenge to cover himself).

He shakes the coin-filled trophy replica — *schlink-schlink-schlink*. A flake of dried spittle flies from his scabbed lower lip as he rhymes:

The Blue and White will win tonight.
and everything will be all right.
Our Leafs will win for me and you!
In Jersey, all will cry "boo-hoo!"

Most of the hockey-sweater-wearing faithful step around him, as if he is a fire hydrant or some other sidewalk obstacle.

A small child waving a "Go Leafs Go!" banner ambles toward the dusty man, burbling and smiling, but her mother tugs her in the opposite direction, scolding, "No, Amberlindzy! Dirty! No!" As they rush toward the safe haven of the arena, the mysophobic mommy frantically digs inside her purse for a bottle of Safety First!™ antibacterial hand sanitizer (with Aloe Vera).

The Plastic Cup Prophet spots two likely marks: a man and a teen. The man is tall and wears a windbreaker with a crest on the chest that reads FAIREVILLE MEMORIAL ARENA; the words ARENA MANAGER are embossed on one sleeve, AARON on the other. Arena Manager Aaron is pushing a kid in a wheelchair, who is wearing a Faireville Blue Flames hockey jersey with a ceremonial team captain's *C* stitched onto the front and WHEELIE embossed on the back. Out-of-towners, for sure, so the Prophet continues, undaunted:

Listen, Arena Manager Aaron! Listen, Captain Wheelie!
The Blue and White like clouds and sky!

You have got to dig this fact.
The Maple Leafs are the children of the trees,
the trees which make the air we breathe.
Air and sky keep us alive, my friends!
All hail the Blue and White!

For his effort, and perhaps for a bit of good karma, Arena Manager Aaron tosses two loonies into the surrogate Stanley Cup, and Captain Wheelie ups the ante with a crumpled five-dollar bill. The Prophet's cup overfloweth, and he holds it overhead, skating circles on holey sneakers around the concrete sidewalk rink.

Then, like a preacher man who's seen the light or the Lord, he lowers the surrogate cup inches from the contributor's face, taps a bony finger on the blue gas-flame crest of Wheelie's bush-league hockey sweater, and chants:

How did they manage to come this far
after barely making the playoffs?
Divine intervention, my man!
God wants the Maple Leafs to win,
to beat those devils, those Jersey Devils.
The Lord is in the Leafs tonight.
They beat the Senators in four straight.
Do you know why?

"Hey!" Arena Manager Aaron protests. "Don't you diss my Senators!" But the Plastic Cup Prophet doesn't miss a beat:

'Cause senators are politicians!
The goodness of nature will triumph
over the artifice of politics!
The Senators wear red and so do the Devils.

The Senators fell, and so will those Devils.
Those Devils from Hell.

"I know it's the playoffs and all," another grinning, adrenalin-charged fan says, "but do you really think God is gonna get involved in a hockey game, dude?"

The Plastic Cup Prophet stretches one Reaper-like finger toward the blue maple leaf crest on the fanboy's Officially NHL-Licensed Toronto Maple Leafs Home Game Jersey, and like any clean-shaven, cologne-wearing, north Toronto McMansion dweller would do, he instinctively takes a step backward.

A carload of teens sail by in someone's daddy's BMW convertible, their faces painted blue and white, their "Go Leafs Go!" banner held aloft; they cheer, "WHOOOOOOOOOO!"

The Prophet flashes a yellowed, gap-toothed grin and says:

They cheer, my man, they cheer,
because they feel the power of the Lord
through the Maple Leafs!
And so shall you cheer as well.
So how 'bout some change, my man?

Mr. North Toronto waves his open palm and reflected streetlight from the man's silver ring glints in the Prophet's eye, so he says:

No change to go ching?
Hey, I'll take that ring!

That ring is the man's lucky charm, though. Whenever he wears it, good things happen. The Leafs are going to win tonight. He's bet good money on it, at ten-to-one odds. Mr. North Toronto retreats, leaving a wake of cologne floating in the air.

The Prophet will not chase after a retreating mark, so jangling the change in his makeshift Stanley Cup — *schlink-schlink-schlink* — he heads toward another knot of approaching pilgrims, chanting:

The Blue and White will win tonight,
and everything will be all right.
Our Leafs will win for me and you!
In Jersey, all will cry "boo hoo!"

* * *

Now it is three hours later. The third period has ended. The game is over.

Six thousand faithful shake their hanging heads. Six thousand pairs of lungs exhale long, anticlimactic sighs. Six thousand pairs of feet shuffle from the temple.

The story, as told through the vessel of the Sony Jumbotron:

The Leafs scored first in New Jersey, but the Devils answered with five goals. *Five freakin' goals!*

And so, the Toronto Maple Leafs' improbable playoff run has ended. Across Toronto, across Ontario, and even in places beyond this realm, thousands of blue-and-white jerseys will be folded up and put away for the summer.

There's always next year. Faith is Faith.

Not too far from the old Maple Leaf Gardens, inside a grimy little diner on Dundas Street, an ancient black-and-white television hangs from above the breakfast bar, broadcasting the closing commentary on *Hockey Night in Canada*, the only program that the diner shows with the volume turned up.

The Plastic Cup Prophet sits at a table in the back corner; the management won't allow him a table in front by the window. Bad for business, they say.

He wipes clean his second bowl of chili with a dinner roll and then drains another cup of thick black coffee. He sighs and rasps through the gaps in his teeth:

Best damn meal I've had in a month.
All hail those Leafs. All hail those Devils.

Impact

im-pact

ˈimˌpakt

1. The action of one object coming forcibly
into contact with another
(as a rocket striking the Earth).
2. Have a strong effect on someone or something.

THE RECEPTIONIST

As the limousine cruises north up Yonge Street, James Yeo feels like the rock star he once thought he might become. He watches the women and girls on the sidewalks; they have traded their long coats and warm boots for low-cut tops and short skirts. They have put on their high heels and they've let their hair down. He's glad that he had his sunglasses in his jacket pocket.

After so many months of stone-grey skies, the intense sunlight makes the whole city seem surreally bright. The sleepy-sounding announcer on the radio refers to the heat as "thermonuclear"; James thinks that this might be overstating it a bit, but then he remembers that this is Toronto, where the news media once named a four-inch snowfall "Snowmageddon."

The radio plays a Valium-mellow version of Jimmy Cliff's "I Can See Clearly Now," and the singer's oozing voice reminds James of melting marshmallows.

James leans forward and says to the limousine driver, "Hey, how about you turn the dial to the Mighty Q, my brother! And crank it!"

"Pardon me, sir?"

The driver's black suit is crisply pressed, and the bill of his chauffeur's cap shines as brightly as his patent leather shoes. The brass plaque on his lapel reveals that his name is Carl.

"Carl, my man," James says, in a classic rock DJ voice, "one-oh-seven-point-one on your FM dial, *s'il vous plaît.*"

Carl wants to roll his eyes, but his Code of Professional Conduct prevents him from doing so. His boss, Harry Riskey, has told him about James, about how Harry's going to "put the loser on the ejector seat" as soon as "he gets some baby batter" into his daughter's "inheritance oven."

"I'm sorry, sir," Carl intones, "Mr. Riskey prefers that the radio remain at a low volume, tuned to the easy-listening station."

"Aw, c'mon, Carl! What Harry doesn't know won't hurt him! Just flip it back to Foot-in-the-Grave FM after you drop me off."

Carl sighs and reaches for a button on the tuner.

Predictably, Steppenwolf's "Born to Be Wild" thunders through the car's premium sound system. James drums along with his fingers on the back of the front seat headrest, and he's filling his lungs to belt out the anthemic chorus when Carl pushes the power button and the song dies a sudden death.

"Yonge and Eglinton," the driver says. "Your destination, sir."

Carl gets out and opens the passenger door for James, who hands him a folded five-dollar bill and then bounces and jives up the sidewalk toward the doctor's office, singing, *"Ah nevahhh wannah DIII-EEEE-IIIIIIIIIIIIE!"*

Carl slides back into the limo, tosses the five on the seat beside him, and says, "At least I make more than he does."

All of the plastic seats in the waiting room are occupied by other patients, so James leans on the check-in counter just inside the door. The receptionist hasn't even noticed him yet. The phone rings, and she grabs it before it can sound a second time.

Doctor Brown, who looks like he might be younger than James himself, bursts into the waiting room.

"Is it time?" he yelps at the receptionist. "Is it time?"

"Not yet," she says, sighing. "I'll come and get you if there's any news. Okay?"

The doctor turns on his heels and retreats into the examination room.

When the call is finished, the receptionist finally acknowledges James's presence by saying, "Name?"

"Um, James. James Yeo."

James's hormones have already been supercharged by the sunshine and short skirts outside, and this effect is multiplied exponentially by his proximity to the attractive receptionist. He doesn't remember seeing her on his first visit to Doctor Brown's office; he definitely would remember her. He is taken by her soft voice with its slightly rural accent; today she's dressed for the weather in a scoop-necked sundress, and as she leans forward on her elbows, James finds something else about her to admire.

"Health card number?" she asks, without looking away from her computer screen.

He fumbles for his wallet, and as he pulls out the requested card, several others fall out. They fly everywhere as he tries to catch them. He stoops to pick them up, and his sunglasses slip from his collar and clatter on the tiled floor. When James finally stands upright again, he offers the cute receptionist his Star Trek fan club membership card.

"It's okay," the receptionist giggles, "I've already found your number on the computer." She finally looks at him with summer-blue eyes. "Sorry about the wait. Doctor Brown's wife's due date was last week, and every time the phone rings, he runs out here. It's slowed things down a little."

James inhales deeply through his nostrils; *she smells like lavender.* She leans forward on her elbows again. James can see her sheer, light-purple bra.

"We are *so* backlogged," she sighs, glancing at the packed waiting room. "The pipe is about to burst!"

Gawd, James muses, *I am so backlogged. MY pipe is about to burst.* He thinks about Sidney pushing him away again this morning, then steals another glance at the receptionist's cleavage. A crucifix and a silver ring, suspended from a slender chain, are nestled between her breasts.

Maybe the ring means she's married, too, James thinks, vividly imagining a vigorous extramarital hotel-room tryst. He can almost feel that ring and crucifix dangling against his face. *Providing a sample won't be a problem today.*

"My name's Clementine, by the way."

"Hi, Clementine," James says.

"Hey, has anyone ever told you that you look just like another James? There was this musician named James Why. He used to play the clubs a couple of years ago, when I was still in nursing school."

"Yeah, I get that a lot," James says.

Actually, James *never* gets this; Clementine is the first person outside his circle of friends to ever mention his former musical alter ego in a non-deprecating way.

"So," James says, drumming his fingers on the desktop, "you're a nurse? How come you're working the reception desk?"

"Nursing jobs are scarce right now," she says, taking note of his wedding ring. "It's a lot more expensive in the city than it was back home, and I'm a single mom with an eight-year-old kid."

She's dropped the Poor Single Mom bomb, and now she is staring obviously at the wedding ring on his finger, but James continues to smile at her. So Clementine smiles back at him.

Doctor Brown bursts into the waiting room again.

Clementine sighs. "I *told* you I'd come get you as soon as —"

"Is this Mr. Yow?"

"It's pronounced *Yeo*, Doctor Brown," Clementine says.

Doctor Brown squints at a chart inside a folder, the way that doctors do, and mutters, "I'd better take you now. Follow me, Mr. Yow."

"It's Yeo," James says. "As in, 'yo, yo, daddy-o!'"

Doctor Brown subtly rolls his eyes. "Right, right, sorry," he grumbles. "Can't read my own damn writing."

Or maybe he said "handwriting." Doctor Brown is difficult to understand when he's mumbling, which is most of the time.

The other patients moan and sigh as James follows the doctor into the examination room. Their glares betray their collective complaint: *This guy strolls in wearing Ray-Bans, flirts shamelessly with the receptionist, and then he gets to jump the queue? Who does he think he is?*

James answers their glares with a dismissive glance, which says: *I'm James Why. I came in a limo. I sing and play the guitar. And ah nevahhh wannah DIII-EEEE-IIIIIIIIIIIIE!*

On the countertop, there are boxes of latex gloves and generic tissues. The concrete-block wall is painted that Digestive Tract Bile shade of greenish-yellow only ever seen in medical facilities, and hanging from it is a blood-pressure-reading apparatus and an empty Dixie cup dispenser. Other than the industrial-sized squirt-bottle of K-Y Personal Lubricant, the only thing that distinguishes the fertility doctor's examination room from any other is that, instead of the usual six-month-old *Time* and *Golf Addict* magazines, there are stacks of *Ass Master*, *Juggs*, *Biker Mamas*, and *MILF International*, as well as a few back issues of *Playboy* and *Penthouse* for those with more refined tastes.

James understands that he is more or less contractually obligated to impregnate Sidney, and that even when he's *imagining* having sex, he is supposed to imagine being inside of *her*, and no one else. He usually pictures her in the kind of provocative poses that she never agrees to assume for him anymore, draped in the kind of sexy lingerie that she never wears for him anymore, saying the sort of enticing things that she never says to him anymore, and usually the hydraulic pressure builds up right away.

But this isn't going to work today. There is an endless, discouraging loop playing on his mind's soundtrack, of Sidney sighing, "For gawd's sake, James! No time for *that*.... For gawd's sake, James! No time for *that*...." and projected on his mind's movie screen is an image of his wife gazing longingly at a texted digital photograph of the Red Buffoon's gold-encrusted dessert, which causes James's equipment to shrivel into a humiliated nub.

James knows that he has a job to do, though, so he will rise to the occasion by thinking about Clementine instead. He will imagine her atop the reception desk, the hem of her sundress tugged up to her waist, her lavender-coloured panties draped sassily over her computer screen, her jet-black Velcro strip invitingly exposed. "Yes, James," she will say. "I want you. Take me. Take me right here, in front of everyone."

James knows that this scenario is ridiculous, but it's *his* fantasy, and this time it will go the way that *he* wants it to go. He is pretty much ready to get started *now*.

While Doctor Brown stands and squints at the contents of the file folder, James sits atop the examination table, listening to the sheet of sanitary paper crackle beneath his butt, and to the plain-faced clock ticking on the greenish-yellow wall: *tick ... tick ... tick ... tick*.

"So," James jokes, "do you want me to strip down and put my feet in the stirrups?"

"Ha ha," mumbles the doctor. "No." He clears his throat and continues to study the charts.

James wonders if perhaps he should open a decade-old copy of *Playboy*, just to pass the time. For the timeless articles they publish, of course.

"Mr. Yow," Doctor Brown finally says.

Instead of correcting the doctor's pronunciation again, James says, "You can call me James."

"James, I've been studying the results of your tests, and there are some indicators here that are somewhat troubling."

"Somewhat troubling?"

The doctor flips some pages.

"Your blood test shows, and your urine and semen tests confirm, that you have a rather rare condition called —"

Inside James's jacket pocket, his Riskey and Gamble–issued phone plays a ring tone version of Queen's sports arena anthem, "We Are the Champions." Harry has warned James to change it back to the phone's standard, businesslike chime, but James hasn't managed to do it yet.

Doctor Brown glances up at the hand-lettered sign taped to the Digestive-Tract-Bile wall, which reads:

PLEASE TURN YOUR CELLPHONE OFF.

The word *off* has been outlined several times in black marker.

"Go ahead," the doctor sighs. "Answer it."

"Uh, hi, Harry," James says into the phone. "Actually, I'm with the doctor right now. Can I call you back? Okay. As soon as I know. Yes. Right away. Okay, then. Don't worry, my sperm is in good hands."

James switches off the phone and tucks it back into his jacket pocket. The doctor glares at James as if he just passed the most rancid of gasses, and James wonders what compelled him to make that last ridiculous comment.

"Sorry," James says. "That was my father-in-law. The one who made my first appointment with you, actually. He's a bit —"

Clementine the receptionist bursts through the door.

"I just got the call," she pants, "It's time for you to go now, Doctor."

The doctor wriggles out of his white lab coat and tosses it atop the stack of *Ass Master* and *Juggs*, and then he sprints out into the hallway. Clementine rushes out behind him. Then their footsteps halt. Doctor Brown mumbles something.

"One month?" Clementine says.

"Her mess," the doctor mumbles. Or maybe he said, "Or less." Then he mumbles something else that James cannot decode.

"No way," Clementine yelps. "No way! That's *your* job, not mine. That's why *you* make the big bucks."

More mumbling, something about "not today of all days." Then a door slams.

Clementine shuffles back into the examination room.

"Hi there," she says, refusing to look James in the eyes. She's holding the folder that Doctor Brown had been squinting at. "The doctor has been called away. Is there any chance we could reschedule your appointment for next week?"

"Have I only got a month to live?"

Clementine looks at the floor tiles.

"I'm sorry, but due to doctor-patient confidentiality rules, only Doctor Brown can —"

"Have I only got a month to live?"

"I can schedule another appointment if you like, for as soon as possible. I really am sorry."

"Am I dying?" James says to himself. Then to Clementine: "Am I dying?"

Dark clouds drift into Clementine's sky-blue eyes.

"I'm sorry," she says

Inside James's jacket pocket, his Riskey and Gamble–issued BlackBerry chimes "We Are the Champions."

James doesn't answer.

And then, underneath the doctor's discarded lab coat, beneath the stack of *Ass Master*, *Juggs*, *Biker Mamas*, and *MILF International* magazines, James sees the spine of a hardcover book:

YOU DESERVE BETTER!
YOU DESERVE MORE!
Rule the Boardroom! Rule the Bedroom! Rule the World!

For some reason, this is the detail that starts James crying.

"Hey," Clementine says, "do you want a hug?"

She crosses the small room and puts her arms around him. Her body is warm. Her breasts feel exactly the way that James imagined they would. He cries even harder.

"Clementine," he says to her, "you were right. I *am* James Why."

Her lower lip quivers, and she sighs. "You were really good, you know."

James feels an invisible noose tightening around his neck. His feet dangle from the examination table.

Was really good. *Was.* Already in the past tense. Already gone.

ROYAL BLOOD

Beneath the iron arches of the bridge that spans the Rosedale Ravine, the Queen hisses and wags a finger at the interlopers.

"Git outta here, you thieving vultures! Shoo! Shoo!"

The raccoons stop and gaze at her for a moment, like teenagers preparing to ignore an ineffective substitute teacher; then they return to their task of ripping into the plastic bag and casually gnawing on the leftovers that the Queen salvaged earlier from the Dumpster behind that diner on Dundas Street.

"Git, you masked bandits! Git! Git! Git! Shoo! Shooooooooo!"

This time, the raccoons don't even look at her. Toronto raccoons are notoriously brazen; they look upon humans as nuisances, not threats.

It occurs to the Queen that she sounds like a scolding mother, and wild animals, no matter how tame they seem to be, are not afraid of scolding mothers; they fear hungry predators who will kill and eat them. So she raises her arms in the air, hooks her gnarled fingers like talons, and rushes at the raccoons, releasing a predatory shriek of mythological proportions.

The raccoons amble away, unfazed. There is no reason to stick around, anyway. They've already eaten all the food.

The Queen sighs. She was looking forward to savouring that unbitten quarter clubhouse sandwich with the half pickle. The Queen loves a good deli pickle.

Her stomach snarls, and the hollow, burning pain of hunger radiates through her abdomen.

She wishes that Rhymin' Simon were still here under the bridge with her; Simon surely would have traded some of his food for something from her borrowed Loblaw's shopping cart. Simon was useful to have around.

Just a ten-minute walk from the bridge where the Queen lives, inside a turreted Victorian mansion in South Rosedale, Tiffany Foley is poking her head through the half-open bevelled-glass doors of her father's den. It's unusual for him to still be home at this hour, so she must take advantage of this rare opportunity.

"Daddy?"

In trying to sound like both the little girl he once adored and the accomplished, academic eighteen-year-old she is now, Tiffany's voice becomes gratingly similar in tone to her mother's pseudo-sexy baby talk. She tries again, using the serious, all-business tone that works so well with her teachers at the Ladycrest Preparatory Academy for Girls.

"Daddy?"

Behind his custom-built desk, with the eagle talons for feet, Stringfellow Foley paces back and forth over the gleaming hardwood floor (which is hand polished weekly by their live-in maid). He raises a finger in his daughter's direction and then continues bawling into the phone.

"Look, it's too late for that, Baldy. We're already building a strategic ring of fire around the vulnerable target securities, understand? You gotta just trust me on this one. Just sit back and wait it out, okay? It's String you're talking to, remember? Just trust me."

Tiffany's father, Stringfellow Foley, a.k.a. "String," is a founding partner of Bloodstone-Talon Capital. His firm specializes in what he describes as "Active Distressed Investing," but the bankers and lawyers in his Scotch-tasting club are more blunt about it; they call Bloodstone-Talon a "vulture fund."

When she was ten years old, Tiffany Foley Googled the term. One website explained it as "a fund that buys securities in distressed investments, such as high-yield bonds in or near default, or equities that are in or near bankruptcy." At the time, she wasn't sure what any of that meant, but she was alarmed by the description that followed the definition.

"As the name implies," the website read, "these funds are indeed like vultures, patiently circling their injured prey, waiting to pick over the remains of a rapidly weakening company. The goal is high returns at bargain prices. Some people look down on vulture funds because they buy up the debts of struggling companies for pennies on the dollar, then they force these companies to pay back the full value of the debts, plus interest."

Tiffany's mouth hung open as she read one of the entries in the website's comments section: "A vulture fund bought the debts of my dad's business and then sued him for the full value of the debt. After my father went bankrupt, he drowned himself in a motel room bathtub. Enjoy your blood money now, you bastards. You won't be able to take it with you to hell."

When Tiffany confronted her father about it all, he simply shrugged and said, "Don't believe everything that you read on the Internet, sweetie, especially in the comments section. Any anonymous rube can say anything there." That reassured Tiffany somewhat, and she wishes now that he had stopped right there, but her father continued, raising his chin, inflating his chest, reciting in his most polished speech-giving voice, "Never feel badly for the losers, Princess. It's the way of the world: Winners win, and losers lose. You have to decide which one you're going to be, and be it."

These words (minus the term "Princess") are the opening lines of Stringfellow Foley's bestselling book on business success, but Tiffany understood her father's philosophy of life a long time before the book was published. Once, when she was four years old and their family was enjoying a beach vacation, Tiffany found a silver ring while digging in the sand. She brought it to her father so he could take it to the resort's lost-and-found office, but her father simply slipped the ring onto one finger of a hand already festooned with huge, glimmering rings, and said "Finders keepers, losers weepers."

The inside of the ring was engraved with the words *Forever More*, and Tiffany has always wondered if the ring somehow influenced the title of her father's book, embossed on the cover in bold, three-dimensional, gold-toned capital letters:

YOU DESERVE BETTER!
YOU DESERVE MORE!

Everything Tiffany's father says is always in big, bold, three-dimensional, gold-toned capital letters, at least in the minds of the up-and-coming Alpha Male Business Champions who read his words like Holy Scripture. Practically every twenty-something, Brooks-Brothers-suit-wearing wannabe on Bay Street owns a copy of her father's book.

The book's royalties paid for their family cottage in the Kawarthas, which Stringfellow Foley has not had the time to visit in years. Every time Tiffany dives from the dock into the cool, clear water there, she thinks of that other girl's father, with his face under water in that motel room tub.

The Queen's final memory of Rhymin' Simon is of him lying face down in the sewage-tainted mud of the Rosedale Ravine.

Just before that, he had poked his dirty face through the little arch in the bridge, near the abutment that the Queen calls home. He bobbed his wild mane of dreadlocks and rhymed:

Your domain, may I enter it,
my sov'reign queen, Elizabeth?

Everyone calls her the Queen, but not just because her name is Elizabeth; she *demands* to be called the Queen. She has a vague recollection that she might once have been someone of importance, so she expects people to accord her the respect that she deserves. She's got Royal Blood pumping through her veins.

Nobody knows the Queen's last name; none of the other ragged loners who live in the ravine, none of the burly, tired cops at the police station, none of the sunken-eyed night-shift nurses in the emergency room, none of the social workers at the women's shelter where she sometimes sleeps when the nights get cold enough to kill.

Not even Elizabeth knows her last name. She can't remember it. She has blocked it from her mind. It was all too terrible. Too terrible to remember. It's impossible to sleep, or even to keep living, when you let yourself remember things like that.

Rhymin' Simon rephrased:

Wont'cha please allow me in,
my benev'lent sovereign?

The Queen remembers this. She has decided not to block Rhymin' Simon from her mind. Remembering him hurts, but it's the kind of hurt that she is strong enough to carry.

"You may enter, Rhymin' Simon," the Queen decreed.

Once he ducked under the bridge, she could see it, tucked under Simon's leathery, bone-thin arm: the Stanley Cup replica that he had constructed from a dented public washroom garbage can, a tomato-juice tin, and a margarine container. He used this makeshift trophy for collecting change from hockey fans as they entered the arena; he said it was part of the show.

"Kin I have my tin back now?" the Queen said to him. "I need something to put my treasures in."

He tugged apart the pieces of the makeshift trophy and handed her the black-red-and-white Heinz tomato-juice tin, while rhyming:

You may, you may, my most fair queen,
Season's over for the Maple Leafs.
No more dough to be had by the ACC.

"Not your best rhyme," the Queen said to him, raising her regal nose in the air.

The Queen refuses to lower herself to begging for change on the street the way that Simon did. She is a collector; she survives on what she can find and use. Occasionally, her scavenging is mistaken for theft, but the Queen reckons that if she is able to freely take something, it must have been free for the taking in the first place.

When Rhymin' Simon was still around, the Queen was sometimes able to "acquire" things for him that he couldn't buy with his nickels, dimes, and quarters, and sometimes Simon would buy for her what she could not "acquire" for herself. It's not that they were friends, really; they were just useful to each other. And that was why the Queen allowed Rhymin' Simon to share her space beneath the bridge.

Simon didn't think of himself as a beggar, though; he was an entertainer, a busker, a troubadour. He would make you smile in exchange for the coins in your front pocket. In the time of real kings and queens, Simon would have been a minstrel, or a court jester, or maybe even poet to the queen.

She remembers that he tried another rhyme:

Then here's a rhyme that ain't so silly:
I brought the Queen some chili
to ease her growlin' belly.

He handed her a Styrofoam bowl filled with chili, and as she dug into the lukewarm feast with her fingers, the Scavenger Queen decreed to her Beggar Poet, "That's better rhymin', Simon."

Simon laughed in that raspy way of his, and then he started coughing; long, wet, bloody coughs, which hurt even to hear. The Queen had tried to get Simon to go see a doctor the last time the outreach workers came around, but Simon had refused. "If I go into a hospital," he had said, "I ain't ever comin' back out again."

So Simon kept coughing, and he kept on coughing until he couldn't breathe.

And then he stopped breathing.

He fell to his knees and keeled over onto his side.

The Queen has a difficult time walking without her borrowed Loblaw's shopping cart to lean on, so she wasn't able to move fast enough to help Simon in time.

Simon's body rolled down the slope of the Rosedale Ravine until he stopped with a splash, face down in the shallow, mucky water.

There was no way that she could make it down the bottom of the valley, so the Queen wheeled herself up to the surface and began screaming and ranting until finally a cop showed up, who then called for an ambulance.

But it was too late. Simon was gone.

The Queen wishes that she could have cried for Simon, but Elizabeth ran out of tears a long time ago, and queens don't cry in public, anyway.

She misses Rhymin' Simon, though. They were useful to each other.

The subtitle of Stringfellow Foley's book is:

Rule the Boardroom! Rule the Bedroom! Rule the World!

Tiffany's father most definitely rules the boardroom at Bloodstone-Talon; he is also a ruthless, dictatorial force within the walls of any company in which his fund has "acquired" control. Although he would never consider wasting his precious time running for any public office, String is in command of so much money (on paper, anyway) that he believes that he is one of those few, rare men who are manifestly destined to rule the world

As for "Ruling the Bedroom," though, Tiffany knows that it has been a long time since Stringfellow Foley has been inside the master suite that he theoretically shares with his wife, Tiffany's mother. On the nights when String manages to come home at all, he sleeps in the basement bedroom of their Rosedale mansion, across from the enormous wine cellar and the tiny maid's suite. Most nights, though, he sleeps in a top-floor suite in the luxury hotel next to his office tower, which Bloodstone-Talon rents on an ongoing basis.

Perhaps, Tiffany supposes, her father still *does* "rule the bedroom" when he's staying at the Royal York Hotel. She has seen that eager glimmer in the eyes of his personal assistant and the female junior associates at Bloodstone-Talon; she can almost *smell* their arousal. Tiffany tries not to think too much about it; he is her father, after all.

Tiffany's mother has had locks installed inside the double doors of the master suite, which she bolts every evening at midnight.

"If he wants *innnn*," her mother says, placing special emphasis on the word *in*, like her idol Joan Collins would do, "then he'd better be home before I lock the doors."

Brandy Foley would enjoy the drama of her husband kicking open the boudoir doors to get to her, to ravage her in that PG-rated way that women get ravaged in the soap operas she spends all day watching, but Stringfellow Foley hasn't been upstairs in the past six months.

When Tiffany's parents first got together, String was an associate at a third-tier firm, and Brandy Brown was one of the receptionists. It was Brandy's first and only job; she would never have to work again after she became Mrs. Foley. At cocktail receptions and expense-account dinners, String very much enjoyed telling others that his wife had been a beauty pageant winner, and when they moved into the Rosedale mansion, he displayed Brandy's Miss Theodore Buttermilk Festival Pageant sash and crown in a glass case in the front foyer, for his whole world to admire.

As String continued to ascend like a rocket up through the corporate stratosphere, parts of his beauty queen wife began to gradually descend. Despite never breastfeeding, Brandy Foley's mammary glands eventually lost some of their bounce, and despite hiring a hundred-dollar-per-half-hour personal trainer, the half-orbs of Brandy's buttocks gradually flattened into mere half-ovoids. Despite ingesting a caloric intake similar to that of the average songbird, Brandy's waistline began to thicken. And Stringfellow Foley's fickle attention began to wander elsewhere.

Brandy fought back, with everything her joint-account platinum credit card could afford. When she caught her husband's gaze lingering on the constantly smiling, aquamarine-eyed receptionist at Bloodstone-Talon, Brandy turned her brown eyes blue with tinted contact lenses, and one-upped the receptionist's sweet smile by plating all of her teeth with tile-white veneers. She paid for collagen injections to plump up her lips, and her eyebrow hairs were removed with a searing laser beam, to be replaced with thin, dark, perfectly symmetrical tattoos of eyebrows. They looked so *real* … until you got up close.

When they were dating, String admired Brandy's cheekbones, which were high and sharp; he said that they reminded him of a 1940s Hollywood femme fatale. So, while Brandy Foley was away on "vacation" in South America, she decided to have them made even higher and sharper. It was a straightforward procedure — just two bits of plastic fused to the bones beneath her eye sockets. It would only take a month or so for the incisions to heal, and she could cover the bruises with makeup in the meantime.

On the same trip, she had some bodywork done as well. By sliding two plastic bags of silicone gel under her skin, the "doctors" at the "clinic" made her breasts firm and round again, two sizes larger than they had ever been. They also looked so *real* … until you touched them. To the fingers, they felt like seamless volleyballs, covered in eerily cool human skin.

A similar process lifted and rounded her buttocks, too, into mathematically perfect half-spheres, and the "doctors" accepted Brandy Foley's money with professionally restrained glee.

To keep the remaining organic components of her body under control, Brandy endures daily cardiovascular workouts with her upgraded two-hundred-dollar-per-half-hour personal trainer, and she substitutes vitamin supplements and protein drinks for eating actual food. Once a year she pays a visit to the liposuction clinic, to have those tiny but stubborn remaining morsels of fat vacuumed out from under her skin. At the same time, after signing the usual waivers, she has her forehead injected with the botulinum toxin; sure, it's one of the most poisonous substances known to medical science, but it paralyzes her muscles and causes her frown lines to temporarily disappear!

Whenever Stringfellow Foley is invited to a “spouse event,” like Patrons’ Night at the Opera House, or some Intergalactic Banking Empire’s by-invitation-only Holiday Extravaganza, Brandy Foley dutifully attaches herself to her husband’s arm, her now-blue eyes sparkling like twin Kashmir sapphires, each pearl-white veneered tooth flashing like La Peregrina. She allows the other traders and investors (with their own quotation-mark nicknames, like Harrison “Harry” Riskey and Baldric “Baldy” Gamble) to gaze down into her surgically enhanced cleavage, displayed to maximum effect by the plunging neckline of her latest shimmering Prada drapery.

Although Brandy behaves exactly as she is expected to behave, which causes the other powerful men in String’s social sphere to covet his wife just the way he wants them to, he nevertheless wears the put-upon expression of a contractually obligated performer.

At the end of such evenings, when the limo brings them home, Mrs. Foley climbs the stairs to the master suite and locks herself behind its massive double doors, and Mr. Foley retreats downstairs to the fifth bedroom. Despite all of the time, effort, money, and risk invested in preserving Brandy Foley’s former-beauty-queen form, there are rarely any attempts at ravaging.

And there will certainly be no ravaging tonight.

Tiffany waits until her father is finished his phone call, and then she says again, more insistently, “Daddy.”

“Just a minute, Princess, okay?” He dials another number, “Yeah, Gunner, it’s me, String. That son of a bitch pulled out at the last minute … yeah, fucking Baldy Gamble. Yeah, yeah, it’s a three-million-dollar shortfall. No, it’s still on … bridge financing, maybe … or maybe we just up the ante on the minor investors, I dunno. Start working the phones, though. Yeah, I’ll be in the office in half an hour.”

He hangs up and begins jamming his rings back onto his swollen fingers. "What is it, Princess?"

Tiffany hates being called "Princess" only slightly more than she hates being called her actual name. What were they thinking when they named her "Tiffany"? It would have been just as subtle to name her "Holt Renfrew" or "Porsche Cayenne."

"Um … well, Daddy … it turns out that I need to have forty hours of community service to graduate this year, and, um —"

"We can get you into business school without all that do-goody-good crap on your resumé," her father snaps. "Mention that I'm your father on the application, and you'll be in. My name's engraved on the patron's wall, for Chrissakes!"

"Well, um, the hours are actually a requirement for me to graduate high school, Daddy."

Her father shoves documents into his Italian leather briefcase. "Aw, don't worry about it, Princess. I'll call the school and demand that they sign off on it. Thirty thousand a year ought to get us that much."

"Well, no, that's not what I want. I thought that maybe you could help me find somewhere to volunteer. Your firm donates to a lot of charities, right? I know you're busy, but maybe you could give me some names, and I can contact them myself."

Stringfellow Foley sighs; if his life depended on it, he couldn't name any one of the charities that his firm donates to. Bloodstone-Talon's accountant takes care of that, mostly to bring the firm's net income down to a lower rung on the tax-bracket ladder.

Cleverly, Tiffany adds, "I was hoping I could count on you, Daddy. Mom hasn't been much help so far."

Stringfellow Foley rolls his eyes at the mention of Tiffany's mother. "I'll get my assistant to make some calls for you, okay?" Then he grabs his briefcase and rushes past his daughter, saying, "Gotta go, Princess. I've got some fires to put out at work."

Just outside the den's double doors, Tiffany hears her mother's Joan Collins voice echoing from the walls of the two-storey front foyer. "Will you be home tonight, *dear*?"

"Not likely," her father says.

Tiffany hovers inside the den; if her mother is about to initiate a battle for marital supremacy, she would prefer to witness as little of it as possible. Witnesses always get called upon to testify later.

Her mind replays an image of her mother with mascara running down her face, pleading to Tiffany with upturned palms: "Is it too much for a woman to want her husband to *be* with her? Am I being unreasonable, Tiffany? Tell me, am I?"

She can also hear her father's barking counterattack: "Who does she think pays all of her bills, Princess? Me, that's who. I've gotta work double time just to pay down her credit cards!"

Tiffany lets out a slow sigh of relief when she hears the front door close as her father leaves them once again.

Then she notices the ring left behind on her father's desktop; Stringfellow Foley has so many, it's easy to lose track of one. It's the silver ring that she found in the sand at the beach when she was a little girl, the one that her father immediately claimed as his own, the only one he wears that isn't made from gold or platinum, the only ring that isn't festooned with diamonds or precious gemstones.

Tiffany plucks the ring from atop the glossy hardwood and slips it into her front pocket. The time has come for her to take it back.

Just a ten-minute walk from the turreted Victorian mansion where the Foleys sometimes live together, the Queen has settled in for the night under the bridge, beside her borrowed Loblaw's shopping cart.

After scanning for raccoons and other scavengers, and after pulling the threadbare tarpaulin over her face, she finally allows the hot tears to cut clean paths through the valleys of her dusty face. Gripped tightly in her right hand is a small, gold-coloured brooch in the shape of a chubby Siamese cat, with a faux ruby for a belly. The gold is only spray paint, and the jewel is just plastic, but tonight this is the Queen's most sacred treasure, the talisman that will pull her through this dark time.

Simon picked it out from inside his begging cup, handed it to her, and said:

Queen Elizabeth One had a Siamese kitty,
and here is another for the Queen of the City.

The Queen misses Rhymin' Simon. They were useful to each other.

HALF-LIFE

Half-life (noun):
The period of time it takes for a substance undergoing decay to decrease by half.

Outside, the air temperature has dropped, and the sky churns smoky grey. There are not many women and girls on the sidewalks now, and the few that remain have tied up their hair, put their long coats back on, and replaced their high heels with tall autumn boots.

James doesn't remember much of his commute home. There is the vague recollection of descending the escalator into the white-tiled glare of Eglinton station and floating through the rush-hour crowd unnoticed, as if he were already a ghost.

When a print ad for some community college assaulted him with the slogan *"It's Your Life!"* from the arched ceiling of the subway car, James shouted back at it, "It *is* my life!"

People moved away and avoided making eye contact with James, so he probably wasn't a ghost just yet. He closed his eyes and almost blacked out. It's a good thing he was holding on to the pole so tightly.

Now, as James stumbles into the tunnel that leads out of York Mills station, he can hear the radio in the ticket booth behind him. In a flat tone, the news reader says, "Today's sudden heavy precipitation and extreme temperature drop represent a record-breaking weather change for the region."

"Record-breaking," James repeats.

He rides the long escalator up toward the surface, but it still feels like he's descending.

No music plays. James Yeo's mental soundtrack has gone silent.

When he reaches the surface, the automatic doors whish open, and wind and rain strike James like a cold-handed slap.

He steps outside, looks for a bus. There are none to be seen. He would flag a taxi, but their top lights are all switched off, their back seats occupied with people wearing that smug *I got here first* expression. There is never an empty cab in weather like this.

James presses forward against the wall of wind as he climbs Wilson Road. The briefcase containing his laptop computer, marked PROPERTY OF RISKEY AND GAMBLE, dangles from his right hand, and a belligerent gust of wind bangs the case against his knees. Razorblade raindrops slice at his face, tears stream from his eyes, and his surroundings become an Impressionistic blur.

A horn blares, and tires hiss against the glazed tarmac as James stumbles from the sidewalk and into the road.

The driver rolls down his window and hollers, "You fuckin' idiot! You wanna die?"

James steps up onto the sidewalk and shouts, "No, I don't want to die!"

It becomes his mantra as he pushes forward, uphill against the rain and wind.

I don't want to die.

I don't want to die.

I don't want to die.

* * *

The alarm panel does not screech when James pushes open the door of the stucco-and-fibreboard McMansion full of Premium Selling Features. He thinks he remembers arming it before he left this morning, but sometimes he forgets. Sidney yells at him when he forgets. *Good GAWD, James! Have some respect for our investment!*

Rain drips from the tip of James's nose, from his earlobes, from his dangling fingertips. Water pools on the mosaic-patterned foyer floor (another Premium Selling Feature).

Does he hear voices upstairs?

James stands still and listens closely.

Definitely. He definitely hears a voice. And another.

Thieves. There are thieves in the house! They've disarmed the alarm, and now they are upstairs, probably rooting through Sidney's jewellery.

James's jaw clenches and his eyes narrow. His vision refocuses, from a ghostly, brink-of-death blur to predatory sharpness.

You picked the wrong fucking house on the wrong fucking day, fuckers.

He drops the *Property of Riskey and Gamble* laptop case on the floor, shrugs off his sopping sports jacket, and steps out of his saturated loafers. He will sneak up on them, take them by surprise. His wet socks slap the floor, so he tugs them off. Barefoot, like a tribal warrior, he'll slink upstairs, and then …

A weapon! I'll need a weapon.

James's old intramural baseball stuff is still packed in boxes in the garage, so he won't be able to use the bat. He could tiptoe into the kitchen, slide the meat cleaver out of its wooden block … but that could get messy. James would prefer something big and heavy, something that bludgeons rather than slashes, something that will cause bruising rather than bleeding. Even in his adrenalized state,

James fears reprisal from Sidney should he stain the imported rainforest-hardwood floorboards or the heated mosaic tiles with the blood of the intruders.

The snow shovel! It's still leaning against the sandstone wall outside. James hasn't put it away yet. Sidney has already yelled at him about it.

James reaches outside and grips his weapon of choice, then gently pulls the door closed. As he tiptoes toward the stairs, his mental soundtrack starts playing again; Joan Jett's "I Love Rock 'n' Roll" thunders inside his cranium. James doesn't know why his brain chose this particular song, but he doesn't have time to think about it right now.

As he reaches the second-highest step of the grand spiral staircase (another Premium Selling Feature), James can feel his pulse throbbing in his grip around the shovel handle.

Prepare to die, fuckers.

"Come on, *fuck me*, Baron!" one voice says.

"*Ohhhh*, those panties are *sweeeeeet*," says the other.

James's breath catches in his throat. His grip on the snow shovel loosens.

"Valentine's present from James," she says. "They dig in a bit."

"Oh, that makes them even better."

"What? That James gave them to me? Or that they dig in?"

"Both."

"You're so *baaaad*," she giggles. "Want to see what's underneath?"

James's vision blurs again. He sways back and forth atop the penultimate stair.

"Oh! Oh! Oh!" Roland Baron cries out. "Bald as an eagle! *Jussssst* the way I like it!"

"You know bald eagles aren't actually *bald*, right?" Sidney says. "They have feathers."

"Bald as a little girl, then," the Red Baron counters.

"Not sure I like that, either."

"Oh, yeah? Well, let me do something that you *will* like ..."

James hears giggling, and then fabric slipping, and he wonders if the three-thousand-dollar duvet cover and dry-clean-only sheets have fallen on the floor.

"Hey, what ... where are you taking me?" Sidney yelps.

"Out onto the balcony," wheezes the Red Buffoon, "We're gonna do it *Romeo and Juliet* style!"

"No no no no no no no! It's right over the driveway! What if James comes home?"

What if James comes home? Now he understands. She *wants* him to catch them, to confront the Red Buffoon, to save her, to be Her Hero once again.

"Come on, baby," Roland Baron says. "It's *romantic.*"

"It's dangerous," she says, in that scolding tone that James has heard many, many times before.

"Dangerous is *sexy*," the Red Buffoon rasps.

James grips the handle of the snow shovel and steps up onto the top floor landing. As soon as Sidney says "No" once more, as soon as she cries out for help, James will run right in there and clang the Red Buffoon on the back of the head. James will save her, and everything will be okay.

But Sidney doesn't say no. She doesn't cry out for help.

What she says is this:

"Ohhhhh ... okay. Let's do it, Romeo. It's the year of living dangerously, right? Grab another condom, though."

"I'll bring *three*!"

Through the bedroom doorway, James can see their backsides, his hairy and hers smooth, reflected back at him from the mirror on the Mission-style dresser, which was a wedding present from James's parents. It has been in the family for five generations. Both of James's parents cried when they handed it over. Sidney never thought it quite fit the décor and has been planning to replace it with something else, something more *chic*, ever since.

In the mirror's reversed image, James watches his wife and his nemesis scamper toward the bevelled-glass doors and out onto the balcony.

James can't look, but he can't look away.

Sidney leans over the balcony, her hair rippling in the light breeze.

The Buffoon barks like a drill sergeant cliché, "Who's the Red Baron?"

"You are!"

"And who's the Red Baroness?"

"I am!"

"Oh, yeah! Oh, yeah! Yeah yeah yeah yeah yeah!"

"Oh … oh oh oh oh … oh, damn! Oh, damn!"

When the Red Baron starts singing an out-of-breath, off-key version of Queen's "We Are the Champions," James decides that he has seen and heard enough.

In the kitchen, there is a used condom draped over the edge of the quartz-topped kitchen counter. James picks up a torn-open gold-foil packet from the floor.

"Ribbed for her pleasure," he reads. "Spermicidal lubricant."

There is also a note, written in Sidney's impeccable handwriting:

Don't forget to go to Priya's place tonight!

DON'T FORGET!

James folds the note in quarters and tucks it into his right front pocket, then, between the thumb and finger of his right hand, he twists his wedding band back and forth until it pops over the knuckle of his ring finger.

James never liked this ring; it's the same sort of huge, gold-and-platinum, jewel-encrusted, attention-seeking sort of thing that Harry would wear, which wasn't surprising, given that Harry had chosen it for James.

The ring clanks atop the quartz where Sidney's note had been, beside the empty gold-foil condom packet. Maybe Roland will like it.

James drifts into the foyer and wipes up the puddles of rain-water from the mosaic-patterned floor. He reaches into the closet, retrieves his comfy hiking boots and his battered old leather jacket, and puts them on. He places the snow shovel back outside the front door.

And then, before the prints of his toes have evaporated from the steps of the spiral staircase, James Yeo is gone.

YOU DESERVE BETTER! YOU DESERVE MORE!

Normally he sleeps right through it, but tonight Keegan Thrush is rattled into consciousness by the noise of the morning train thundering past beneath the window. Atop the bedside table, the digits on the alarm clock glow red:

8:11 a.m.

If she were awake right now, she would get all excited about that. Lately she's moved from astrology to numerology, or whatever. Atop the nightstand on her side of the bed (well, technically *both* sides of the bed belong to *him*) sits the latest pink-flower-festooned soft-cover library book she's reading:

Take Control of Your Life
with
NUMEROLOGY!

If she were awake right now, she would tell him that the glowing red LED number eight is like, *oh my gawd*, the infinity sign turned sideways, and eleven is, *like*, the number of balance and change.

Whatever. She's hot. And she's a fucking *maniac* in bed.

As he rolls over, he says, "Hey, baby, it's eight-eleven. Wanna turn sideways? Or maybe you'd like to balance on top of my … hey, where the hell are you?"

She must be in the bathroom. He flips over, and his bare feet touch the cool white-tiled floor.

"Fine," he says, "I'll come getcha in there."

On his nightstand is the latest hardcover guidebook for Successful Alpha Male Business Champions, written by an author with an unlikely but somehow authoritative name: Stringfellow Foley. The book's title is embossed on the dust jacket in three-dimensional gold letters:

YOU DESERVE BETTER!
YOU DESERVE MORE!
Rule the Boardroom! Rule the Bedroom! Rule the World!

The red glow of the alarm clock illuminates the small square of lavender-coloured notepaper that she has left behind, neatly centred on the book's front cover.

He reaches for the note, which is written in her tight, ornate script.

> *I know what you did.*
> *Did you think that I wouldn't find out?*
>
> *I'll be leaving on a train tomorrow,*
> *and you'll never see me*
> *or touch me*
> *or hear from me again.*
>
> *Goodbye forever,*
> *Emily*
>
> *PS I hope you die and go to hell.*

His system immediately switches into Crisis Containment

mode. He grabs his slick new smartphone and calls her number, his mind racing to invent a believable explanation.

A pre-recorded voice informs him *"The number you have dialled is not in service."*

He grabs the clothes that are lying on the floor, dresses, and sprints for the door. Maybe he can catch her before she leaves, tell her it wasn't what it looked like, that it was all just a big, crazy misunderstanding.

"Fuck that," he says to his translucent reflection on the floor-to-ceiling windows of his condo. There is no "maybe" for men in his position. He lives at the top of the world. He has it all. He *deserves* it all.

From up here, he's got a view of the CN Tower and the Air Canada Centre, where his firm owns platinum season's tickets for the Leafs. He raises both middle fingers and aims them at the Air Canada Centre.

"Fuck you guys!" he says. "I'm better than anyone on your pathetic team."

Keegan was scouted to play for the Leafs and several other NHL teams, but the scouting reports described him as "temperamental," "inconsistent," "uncoachable," and "not a team player," so his father eventually had to call in a favour and get Keegan a job at an investment firm, where he makes as much money as an NHL all-star anyway.

On a clear day, Keegan can see friggin' *Hamilton* from here. It isn't clear today, though; through the falling rain, the towers that surround him are simple geometric blurs. Today his view reminds him of the prints of Impressionist paintings that she's hung all over his condo, to "give it some life."

"Be *vital*!" he commands his reflection. "You *will* catch her at the station. You *will* tell her that she's wrong. And you *will* convince her to come back with you. Be *vital*."

He's about to sprint to the elevator, when something occurs to him. "My ring! My fucking lucky ring!"

When Keegan set the Wheatfield Major Junior Hockey League's (still-unbroken) record for Most Goals Scored in a single game, he and his teammates left the arena immediately to go celebrate at the Ooh La La All-Nude Gentlemen's Club; the stretch limousine, the drinks, and the girls were all paid for by Keegan's father. The next day, when Keegan realized that he had forgotten to claim the puck that hit the twine for his eleventh goal of the game, he raced back to the Faireville Memorial Arena to claim his prize.

By then the puck was long gone, but the arena manager had found a ring on the ice, engraved on the inside with the words *Forever More*. So Keegan claimed that instead.

"Fucking right, Forever More!" he says to himself now. He *does* deserve better. He *does* deserve more. "I am Keegan fucking Thrush, muthafuckahs!"

With his lucky ring in place, Keegan smirks and winks at his reflection again.

"You're the Man in Charge, pal. You're a gunslinger. You're a fucking *gunslinger*."

He tugs his index fingers from their front-pocket holsters, cocks back his thumbs like hammers, and takes aim at his reflection.

The makeup sex is going to be *insane*.

Outside his building, Keegan waves frantically for a taxi, but each one passes him by.

"Shit! I'd give my fucking *life* for a cab right now."

Then, through the hiss of the rain on the pavement, he hears the sore-throat rumble of a V8 engine approaching. As the limousine turns the corner, its engine gets louder, its pitch higher.

He steps onto the road and waves his hand in the air. "Taxi! Taxi!" he shouts.

Inside the car, the driver slumps against the door, his life taken in an instant by a ruptured cerebral aneurysm. His life is over, just like that.

The driver's black suit is crisply pressed, and the bill of his chauffeur's cap shines as brightly as his patent leather shoes. The brass plaque on his lapel reveals that his name was Carl.

The limo veers toward Keegan. He is frozen in place.

The high-beam headlights are like angry eyes. The chrome teeth of the grille are snarling, predatory.

"Get out of the way!" Keegan commands himself, but his body does not obey.

There is the hissing of tires on the wet sidewalk and then a thump, followed by shattering as the limo smashes through the glass-shrouded foyer of the gleaming condominium tower.

And then there is the faint scent of burnt rubber in the thick, damp air. There is the rattle of stray raindrops on the sidewalk, and a sound like fingertips drumming on the metal of the trunk of the car, which protrudes from the building like an undetonated shell.

Some distance from the body of Keegan Thrush, his lucky silver ring jangles on the sidewalk.

She is aboard a train bound for somewhere new, her face pressed against the glass. She watches the scenery race past, backlit by the first orange sunlight of the day. The retreating rain clouds are beautiful; they remind her of the prints of Impressionist paintings that she had to leave behind.

Her heartbeat plays counterpoint to the metallic rhythm of the wheels on the tracks, and she repeats her new mantra, which seems to have entered her consciousness from somewhere beyond this mortal plane:

"You deserve better. You deserve more.

"You deserve better. You deserve more."

She smiles at her reflection in the window, as if she's posing for a new headshot for her portfolio. This photo would be a nice one: *Beautiful Lone Traveller Bravely Begins a New Life.*

For a moment, she wonders if he has found her note yet, and if it has shaken him up at all.

Then she turns back to the image of herself in the window.

Escape Velocity

es·cape ve·loc·i·ty

ɪˈskeɪp vəˈlɒsɪti

The velocity that a moving body (as a rocket) must attain to escape from the gravitational field of a celestial body (as the Earth).

SANGRIA RED AND OCEAN BLUE

James pushes the creaky door open and tiptoes into the foyer of the old house, which is divided from the landlord's domain with nothing but old curtains. The probably senile old guy never remembers James's name, and refers to him as "Priya's repairman." James supposes that this description is apt enough.

When Sidney first sent him over to help Priya with her apartment renovations, the work was pretty demanding:

- Scraping off decades-old, smoke-yellowed wallpaper, inches at a time.
- Patching the holes in the plaster that had been hidden under the decaying wallpaper.
- Tearing up the matted, cat-piss-and-puke-stained carpets to reveal the maple floorboards underneath.
- Sanding off a century's worth of paint layers from the mouldings and banisters to get to the wood underneath, which Priya and James then stained and varnished to its current glorious condition.
- Carrying the practically antique kitchen appliances down the narrow staircase to the curbside and, as Priya could afford them, lugging the new appliances up.
- Filling in and painting over the damage to the staircase wall caused by lugging appliances up and down.

- Painting the walls Priya-style colours: Blackberry-Wine Purple. Spring-Meadow Green. Sangria Red. Ocean Blue.

On the one and only occasion that Sidney stopped by to give her Professional Opinion on their progress, she disapproved of Priya's colour choices.

"Good gawd, James, why didn't you stop her? The place looks like a candy store! Or a playground. Yeah, that's what these colours remind me of! Those indoor playgrounds for kids, with the room full of coloured plastic balls."

The interior of Sidney's North Toronto mansion is finished in neutral, resale-friendly colours: Latte Beige. Hazelnut Beige. Burlap Beige. Wheatfield Beige. Roasted Sesame Seed Beige. Hampton Beige. Butterscotch-Martini Vomit Beige.

(The latter appeared on the bathroom wall after one of Sidney's outings with Roland Baron. James cleaned it up, while Sidney snored "*Rrrrrrroland … Rrrrrroland …*" Ah, the power of denial!)

The voice of Priya's landlord crackles from behind the faded, musty curtains. "Somebody out there? Somebody come to see me?"

"It's me, sir."

"Priya's repairman! Wanna sit a spell and chew the fat, son?"

The old guy is nice enough, and normally James would stop to talk with him. But not today. James needs to see Priya right away.

He pulls open the apartment door that he helped paint (he did the rolling, Priya did the details), and James ascends the staircase, which is so narrow that his shoulders brush both walls as he climbs. He turns sideways to avoid bumping the reproductions of paintings by Manet, van Gogh, and Goya, which Priya once found leaning against a Dumpster in an alley; she has the rare ability to find the value in things that others have abandoned, to transform the discarded and devalued into treasures again.

James needs to see Priya.

She is usually there to greet him at the top of the stairs.

"Priya?" James calls out.

There is no reply.

He looks at the 1940s movie posters that hang in the narrow hallway: *Casablanca. Citizen Kane. Notorious. The Maltese Falcon. An Affair to Remember.* James and Priya have watched all of these films together, sneaking out to the local repertory theatre when they were supposed to be scraping, sanding, and painting. Sidney despises such "boring old stuff," preferring loud, glossy, new Hollywood movies with THX surround sound and CGI and "actors who are still alive."

"Priya?" James calls out again.

Still no answer.

He examines the painting that Priya bought from an elderly couple's yard sale just up the street. She thought that it was a scene from Old Montreal, but James was pretty sure it was Sacré-Coeur in Paris. Priya decided she liked that explanation better, and she paid the old couple five dollars for it, when they were only asking for one.

"I paid *five times* the asking price, and it's *French*," she said. "I now officially own a piece of *real art*!"

James had to laugh at that; Priya was making fun of Sidney's sudden expertise in art. All of the paintings in the McMansion were chosen by an interior decorator hired by Sidney on the strong recommendation of Roland Baron. Directly quoting the three-hundred-dollar-an-hour decorator, Sidney described the two huge new "investment pieces" in her living room as "vibrant abstracts in kinetic teal," and she scolded James when he referred to the colours as "greeny blue" or "bluey green." Like the suddenly insufficient diamond in Sidney's engagement ring, the two paintings cost more than James's first three cars combined.

James still likes Priya's five-dollar painting of Sacré-Coeur better.

"Priya?" James calls out again.

No reply.

The landing at the top of the stairs is almost too narrow for James to turn around. He looks to the right, into the tiny, makeshift kitchen. Priya is sometimes in there making tea when he arrives. She isn't there today.

James looks to the left, down the dangerously narrow hallway; dangerous because it runs parallel to the staircase, divided only by a knee-level railing. Once, when they were on their second can of paint and third bottle of cheap Bordeaux, James took a half-step back to admire his work and nearly toppled ass-first over the railing. He and Priya laughed until they couldn't breathe.

"Hey, Priya! Are you here?"

"I'll be out in a minute," comes Priya's muffled voice from behind the bathroom door. "Make yourself at home."

She must not have heard him earlier. He hadn't noticed that the door was closed; Priya usually forgets and leaves it wide open. She's become accustomed to living alone.

James kicks off his shoes, which are still damp from the earlier downpour, and he shrugs his almost-dry jacket onto the bannister. As usual, Priya's panties and bras and other lacy underthings are draped over the railing to dry after washing, like decorations around the edges of a pubescent boy's wet dream.

(Sidney, by comparison, washes each of her "intimates" one at a time on the delicate cycle of their state-of-the-art washing machine, then she gingerly plucks out each slight item between her index finger and thumb, carrying it to the ensuite to blow it dry with her hair dryer. Then she tucks it into its own Ziploc bag, which she files in her dresser, sorted by style and colour.)

James moves through Priya's tight hallway, careful to tuck in his shoulders to miss the mirror surrounded by seashells and the little framed pictures of white-leather-jumpsuit Elvis, Henry Winkler as the Fonz, femme fatale Bette Davis, and Marilyn Monroe's famous subway grate scene from *The Seven Year Itch*.

As he passes Priya's open bedroom door, he notices the print of Manet's *Un bar aux Folies Bergère*. He had given it to her as a housewarming gift. The pendant around the subject's neck reminds James of the kind of thing that Priya would wear herself, and the woman's dark, slightly disappointed-looking eyes could belong to Priya too.

James supposes that she falls asleep looking at the Manet. This makes him smile a little.

Priya's small living room is crammed with knick-knacks: candles, books, vintage cameras, tiny medicine bottles made of green, blue, and brown glass, kerosene lamps, chrome hood ornaments from antique cars, and other colourful, curious objects that caught Priya's eye at garage sales and second-hand stores.

Priya's place has a turntable, an amplifier, and stereo speakers, with hundreds of real vinyl records in "borrowed" green and blue plastic milk crates. Some of the records once belonged to Sidney, back when she still allowed her friends to call her "Sid," back before she became the "protégée" of Roland Baron.

The music inside Sidney's McMansion comes from a remote-controlled, subscription-service satellite music system; James has never figured out how to convince the system to play the music he actually wants to hear, rather than the "ambient modern trance" that Sidney has selected as the default channel (again on the recommendation of Roland Baron's three-hundred-dollar-an-hour decorator).

James *does* know how to play records, though, so he gets up to put one on the turntable. He selects The Supremes' *Greatest*

Hits, which he and Priya listened to a lot when they were working together on this room.

"Hey!" James calls out. "Are you okay in there?"

Priya, unlike Sidney, is usually in and out of the washroom in under five minutes. Sidney takes over two hours each morning to make herself "perfect."

James corrects himself: Sidney *took* over two hours each morning. Sidney only exists in the past tense now.

"I'm here," Priya says.

She had walked in so softly on her bare feet that James didn't hear her enter the room.

James turns away from the turntable to face her.

The whites of her eyes are bloodshot, her eyelids swollen. Strands of her long black hair cling to her wet face.

"Wow," James says, "what —"

She lunges at him, wraps her arms tightly around his torso, buries her face in the valley between his shoulder and chest, sniffling and sighing.

"You're warming me," she says. "Don't let go."

Priya is wearing her purple terry-cloth bathrobe, which James has seen hanging on the knob of her bathroom door, but never on her body. He doesn't let go.

"This morning," she says, "I felt like there was nothing I couldn't do. I felt like I could change the world today. I felt like I could make it all better." Five staccato inhalations and then, "Things can change so quickly. What a day."

"It *was* a bad day," James says.

"Do you want to tell me about it?"

James shrugs. "You first."

She sighs. "Okay. So, there's this kid at school, Eric, whom I've been counselling for so long … shit! I shouldn't have said his name! Confidentiality! Gawd, what's wrong with me?"

"There's *nothing* wrong with you, Priya," James, says, pushing a strand of hair out of her face. "Tell me about the kid. I forget his name already."

"He's creative. He's sensitive. And he's very, very angry."

She drifts into herself for a moment. James strokes her hair and waits.

"Anyway," she says, "he's been having trouble with his dad at home, arguing, physical confrontations. His father kicked him out, and he's been couch surfing for the past few weeks. So, I invited them both to my office to talk it over, with me as the mediator."

She shivers. James pulls her in a bit closer.

"As soon as they both got into my office, before I even got a chance to say a word, they were screaming at each other. And then they started fighting. And I mean full-out, trying-to-kill-each-other fighting. Punching, kicking, *biting* ... it didn't end until the son threw a big ceramic planter at his father's head. He ducked, and the planter smashed through the window on my office door. Then they both took off."

"Are you hurt?"

"Not physically."

"Did you say there was *biting*?"

"The kid bit his dad's hand. The Father of the Year bled all over my *Official Conflict Resolution Manual*."

"He bled all over your *Official Conflict Resolution Manual*?"

"I guess I should order a new one, eh?" She laughs a little. "The dried blood might send the wrong message in other mediations." She pulls herself closer. "You are so warm."

All James can think to say is, "You can't fix everything."

"But I *want* to fix everything."

James glances around the room, at the dump she's transformed into a home, at the bits of trash she's transformed into treasures.

"I know you do," he says, kissing her forehead. "That's why I love you so much."

"Really? You love me so much?"

He nods.

She stands on her tiptoes, bringing her face closer to his. "Thanks. I need someone to love me today."

She kisses him on the mouth; her body is still shivering, but her lips are warm.

James sucks her upper lip between his, Priya flicks her tongue under his front teeth. Soon their tongues are spiralling together like currents in a whirlpool.

James's hands slip up under her purple bathrobe, up and then down her goosebump-speckled back, gripping the round of her behind.

They fall onto the couch. Priya unties her robe, and James pushes it open, like parting velvet curtains.

Every fantasy he has ever had in the shower about Priya floods through his mind and body. He frantically kisses her neck, her collarbone, sucks her nipples into his mouth, licks into her navel.

Priya arches her back, pulls James's hair, breathes as if she is running for her life.

Then she pushes his face away from her skin.

"Wait!" she cries. "No! We can't."

"We *can*," James says.

"But … Sid! I mean *Sidney*. No. We can't."

James props himself on one knee against the sofa cushion and pushes his fingers into his front pocket, past his aching erection, digging out the note. He unfolds it to show Priya.

Don't forget to go to Priya's place tonight!

DON'T FORGET!

"She's been sending me to your place so she can fuck Roland Baron."

"What? Her … um … *mentor*?"

"I caught her with him tonight."

"*That* guy?"

"In our bedroom. On our bed."

"Oh, James."

"So we can do whatever we want to, Priya. Sidney can go to hell."

James pushes Priya's legs open and descends between them.

Her back arches against the sofa cushions. Little waves ripple through her stomach muscles.

Then Priya pulls herself away from James, crawls out from under him up onto the arm of the sofa. She pulls the bathrobe around her body, steps backward onto the floor, ties the purple terry-cloth belt tight around her waist.

"No, James," she says. "Not like this."

"But Priya —"

"Not like this."

James rises from the couch, reaches for her.

Priya steps back from his outstretched fingers. "I can't be your revenge fuck, James."

"What?" James yelps. "Revenge f—? What?"

Priya is crying again. "I can't be your revenge fuck. I won't. Not after everything else. It has to be more than that."

"Priya, it, it *is* more than that!"

She pulls the bathrobe tightly around her torso, tugs it down to cover anything that might still be exposed.

"James, you have to go. It's been a bad day for both of us, and you have to go now. Okay?"

"Priya —"

"James, you have to go."

"Priya."

"James, you have to go now."

He wants to kiss her as he passes her, only on her forehead, or maybe on her cheek. But he doesn't. Any kind of kiss means something completely different now.

As he recedes clumsily through the narrow hallway, James's hip sends a flock of Priya's lingerie fluttering over the railing. His shoulder bumps femme fatale Bette Davis, knocking her frame crooked against the wall.

As he passes Priya's bedroom, he sees *Un bar aux Folies Bergère*, with that pensive, distant expression on the woman's face. He glances back to see Priya standing in her small, kitsch-jewelled living room; she has the same expression on her face now, too. And James finally understands what it means.

On the cramped landing, he pulls on his hiking boots, tugs his leather jacket around his shoulders. As he descends the narrow staircase, he turns sideways to avoid bumping the salvaged Manet, van Gogh, and Goya reproductions.

He reaches for the doorknob, but then he hesitates, turns around, looks up.

Priya is standing at the top of the stairs.

"I meant to give you something," she says, "before we got carried away."

She tosses something small from the top of the stairs. James catches it with both hands.

It's a ring. A simple silver ring. James holds it up to the single dim light bulb that hangs above his head. The ring is engraved inside. It says *Forever More*.

"I found it on the sidewalk downtown. I thought that you might like it."

"I do."

It nestles comfortably into the groove left behind by his discarded wedding ring, covering that bloodless wound. The ring is maybe a bit loose, but his fingers are cold; it will fit perfectly when things warm up again.

"Thanks."

"You're welcome."

James stands at the bottom of the stairs, and Priya stands at the top.

Finally, she sighs. "*An Affair to Remember*."

"I'm not sure that this qualifies as an 'affair,' Priya."

"The movie," she says. "Remember?"

Of course he remembers. They saw it together at the repertory theatre after putting on the last coats of Sangria Red and Ocean Blue.

They loved that old cinema — the flickering pink neon tubes outside, the burnished brass concession stand, the pastel-coloured paint peeling from the art deco friezes inside the cool, musty womb of that decaying theatre.

Priya had smuggled a mickey of Crown Royal into the mostly empty movie house, and she'd emptied it into the bucket of watery soda-fountain cola they bought at the concession stand. She and James sucked on their wax-paper-cup highball through two red-and-white-striped plastic straws, like kids on a date in a bygone era.

The scent of Priya sitting next to him in those crushed-down velvet seats was more intoxicating than the whiskey. Rather than wearing boutique perfume that costs as much per ounce as precious metals, Priya dabs vanilla extract on the back of her neck and behind each ear. When she leaned against him to sip that rye and Coke, her left breast would brush James's right forearm; James knew that she was wearing that sexy transparent black bra beneath her blouse (he had watched her pluck it from the railing). It took all of his fortitude to prevent himself from kissing her vanilla-scented neck and earlobes.

James looks up at her now, standing there in her purple bathrobe at the top of the narrow staircase.

"I remember," he says.

Cary Grant and Deborah Kerr. They were both engaged to marry other people, but they fell in love with each other anyway. They would meet again in six months at the top of the Empire State Building if their love was meant to be.

"We'll meet at the top of the CN Tower in six months," Priya says. "If we both still feel the same way, we can take it from there. Okay?"

A jolt flashes through James's body. *Six months?* He doesn't have six months. He is not going to play the *I think I might be dying* card now, though; how desperate and pathetic would *that* look? So he simply says, "I don't think I can go six months without seeing you, Priya."

She sucks in her lower lip, the way she does when she's trying not to cry. Even from this distance, from the bottom of the staircase, even in this dim lighting, with her face lowered into a shadow, James can see it.

"Six weeks, then," Priya says. Then, with a flourish of her purple bathrobe, she turns and disappears.

James turns and pushes open the front door, and it sings out that lonesome high note, as always.

From behind the mould-scented curtains, the voice of Priya's landlord crackles like a dusty record. "Priya's repairman! You leavin' now, son?"

"Yes, sir," James says.

"Everything fixed now?" the old man wonders.

"No. Not everything."

James hovers at the foot of the stairs and contemplates ascending.

THE TOES OF ONE FOOT

Dapper Dan's voice scratches the air like 80-grit sandpaper. "You know, Clementine, you can count the number of perfect days in a year on the toes of one foot."

As she wheels the old warrior out from under the awning and into the sunlight, Clementine wonders why he said "the toes of one foot" instead of "the fingers of one hand." At least he is using her actual name today; sometimes she is "Mary," since apparently Clementine reminds Dan of some woman from his war years, where his memory has been spending a lot of time lately.

"Some days are so cold it's cruel," Dan continues, pausing to inhale the fragrant summer air. "And then some days are so hot it sucks the life right out of you. Some days you get soaked with rain, and some days you get pelted with snow and ice."

His tone of voice adds a certain authority to everything he says. It reminds Clementine of a recording of some important speech, delivered through a crackling old radio with the tone knob cranked over to the bass side.

"Some days the wind gets up and tries to knock you down, and some days the air is just too still, like it's waiting to pounce. Some days are so humid the air feels thick and congealed, like a bowl of reheated soup. Some days are so dry your skin cracks and blisters, like an old workboot."

Dan's seasoned, saddle-leather voice makes it seem to Clementine as if he is imparting some ancient wisdom to her, some metaphorically encoded philosophy of life, even when all he is doing is making small talk about the weather.

"But days like this one," he continues slowly, sustaining the note of each vowel, stretching each syllable as if he's playing a jazz solo on a tarnished saxophone, "days like this one are a true rarity."

Dapper Dan and Clementine drift for a moment in the sweet, beautiful silence, until it is shattered by Sheila, the supervising nurse, who clangs the time-change bell as if she's rattling a battlefield sabre. Sheila runs the veterans' wing of the Faireville Nursing Home as if it's a strict military unit, which the facility's former-soldier patients neither want nor need.

Dan chooses to ignore the jangling bell. He says, "We should savour this day, Clementine, to show our appreciation. We should linger in this day, to show our gratitude."

"And to whom should we show our gratitude, Dan?" Clementine says, knowing that Dan has proclaimed himself to be an atheist; she has observed that most old warriors either believe in God completely, or not in much of anything at all.

"We should be thankful to nature, I suppose," Dan says. "Or to the universe, perhaps. Or to chance, maybe. To fate. To luck. To chaos. To whatever force it is that makes anything happen in this world." He turns to glance up at Clementine, who is leaning on the grips of his wheelchair; he knows that his favourite nurse comes from a strictly religious family, so he offers, "Or to God, I suppose, if that's what you choose to call it."

Clementine closes her eyes and draws a long, slow breath in through her nostrils. The sound of her own breathing reminds her that she is alive. She would love to linger all afternoon on the sun porch with Dan, but now Nurse Sheila is screaming at her through the sliding doors of the veteran's wing.

"Gawd-damn mit, Clem! Gawwwwwd-DAMN IT! How many times do I have to call you inside, Clem? Do the rules not apply to you?"

Clementine hates it that Sheila always calls her "Clem." She isn't fond of the name Clementine to begin with, but *Clem* sounds like the name sewn onto the patch on a pair of used worker's overalls in the discount bin at the Sally Ann store. That's probably the way that Sheila sees her, though: as just another labourer.

Sheila is a registered nurse with a university degree, while Clementine only has a college-level licensed practical nursing diploma. Sheila holds this distinction over Clementine's head the way that a duchess might use her title when dealing with a household servant. Clementine has to swallow it, though; Sheila is her direct superior, and she needs this job. Clementine has a son to feed and clothe, so Sheila knows that she is not going to talk back or give her any trouble.

"Come on, Clem, let's move it!" Nurse Sheila screeches. *"You're not a fancy city girl any more. You gotta get your hands dirty like everybody else."*

Clementine used to believe that attending university made one more mannered and sophisticated, but Nurse Sheila's behaviour has crushed that illusion. University degrees don't necessarily make people more moral, either; Clementine was fired from her job in Toronto when a flustered doctor, with multiple degrees hanging in his office, mixed up a couple of patient files and needed someone to blame. Clementine had to come crawling back to Faireville, which was the last thing she ever wanted to do.

Sheila continues, in love with her authority. *"He's scheduled for his bath right now, Clem, not tomorrow! You're putting us behind schedule! Bring that dirty man inside right now!"*

"I like what *any* red-blooded man likes," Dan says, "but I am *not* a dirty man."

"I know," Clementine tells him. "You're a gentleman, Daniel."

She also knows that he is still a "red-blooded man"; she has seen the longing in his eyes as he watches her walk away. Maybe she sways it a little more than usual for him, the way that she suspects women might have done back in the forties, during Dan's most virile years.

Dapper Dan likes it when Clementine calls him "Daniel." He also likes it when she calls him a "gentleman." She is the only person who calls him either anymore.

"Well," he says, "*this* gentleman does not want to be given a bath by *that* cantankerous bull moose." Dan glances up at Clementine again. "Couldn't you do it for me instead? I promise I'll be good."

"Sorry, Dan," she says. "Not allowed, I'm afraid."

The last time she washed Dan, his erection sprang up through the water's skin like a purple-headed sea monster, parting the seas inside the geriatric washtub with Biblical drama.

"Well … well … wow!" the nurse's aide had exclaimed from the other side of the tub. "That is … ummm … that is … truly a medical oddity, isn't it?"

It truly was.

After that, Clementine was permanently excused from bath duty by Nurse Sheila.

"That is indeed a shame," Dan says now, the dark pools of his eyes absorbing the details of Clementine's face: that slight concave imprint above her soft upper lip, her marble-sculpture cheekbones, those cornflower-blue eyes, and her dark eyebrows, arched slightly upward in the middle.

He sighs. *So much like Mary. Mary, Mary, quite contrary. My saviour, Mary.*

And then: *Snap out of it, Daniel. That was a lifetime ago.*

"Well, then," Dan says, smiling up at Clementine again, "if we can't spend any more time together during my bathing ritual, could we perhaps savour this perfect day together for just a minute longer?"

Clementine doesn't mind indulging him, even if it means catching some hell from Sheila. Although he is almost one hundred years old, she likes the tone of his voice and the twinkle in his eyes. She imagines that he was quite a charmer in his day.

Nurse Clementine and Dapper Dan watch the cottony clouds drift past in the surreally blue sky, and they each give their own kind of thanks.

Nurse Sheila's shriek once again pierces the silence like an air-raid siren.

"Gawd-dammit, Clem! Gawwwwwd-DAMMIT!"

And thus the moment is called to an end.

Clementine wheels Dan inside and hands him over to Sheila.

"Tomorrow's my day off, Dan," she says. "See you on Monday, okay?"

Dan watches Clementine's behind sway beneath the skirt of her pastel-yellow nurse's uniform as she walks away.

"You're a good reason to stay alive," Dan says to himself, drifting backward.

Dapper Dan watches the upside-down valentine-heart of Mary's behind lift inside the skirt of her royal-blue uniform as she stands on her tiptoes to reach the top shelf.

"Mmmmmm, Mary," Dan says to her, "you *do* know how to wear a skirt."

"Shhhhhh!" she hisses at him, as flames dance in her blue eyes. "Someone might hear you!"

"Mary, Mary, quite contrary," Dan says, while glancing around the empty room. "There's nobody here but you and me."

"I see they brought some new planes in," she says, in a faux-official tone. "Will you and your crew be flying in one of them? I'd say you boys have earned some new wings."

A handful of newly built Lancasters were indeed delivered to the airfield earlier in the week, and a few of them came equipped with the new Rose Brothers tail gunner's turret. The Rose turret has greater visibility than the usual Nash and Thompson he's become accustomed to, and it's got bigger, .50-calibre guns; those will definitely make a bold statement the next time the nose of a Luftwaffe night fighter drops into Dan's gunsights.

The best thing about the Rose turret, though, is that it's so much roomier inside. For a tall guy like Dapper Dan, it would be like flying first class; folding himself into the cramped Nash and Thompson makes Dan feel like a giraffe in a goldfish bowl. To keep his legs and feet from cramping, Dan sometimes has to take his feet off the footrests and move them around inside the tiny Perspex-and-steel bubble, just to keep his blood circulating.

On the last mission, after they had dropped their load, a Junkers Ju 88 night fighter dropped down right behind the Lancaster, its twin propellers spinning on either side of Dan's peripheral vision, so close that Dan could see the pilot's face. Shells from the Junkers's 20-millimetre cannon streaked past, between Dan's turret and the Lancaster's twin tail fins.

Dan usually fired his Browning three-oh-threes in short, controlled bursts, but the sudden attack jolted him so that he blasted through the nose and canopy of the Ju 88 in a steady, rattling stream, and he kept firing long after the burst of crimson smeared the glass of the pilot's canopy. The Ju 88 finally bucked up in the air like a panicked horse and then disappeared down and out of Dan's sight in a wide arc of oily smoke.

Afterward, Dan's legs were numb from the thighs down. He put his tingling feet up on the guns, only for a moment, but by that time the Brownings were hot enough to cook a steak well done. As it turned out, they were also hot enough to burn the heels off Dan's boots, too. Thanks to the stench of cordite fumes that saturated the air around him, Dan felt the heat on his heels before he smelled the smoke.

So Dan has come to the supply depot counter to get some new boots. It's as good an excuse as any to visit Mary during the daylight hours, too.

On any mission over enemy territory, Dapper Dan spends hours at a time cramped inside that tiny bubble hanging from the tail of the Lancaster, separated from the rest of the crew by closed armoured doors, his only human contact being the intermittent, disembodied crackle of voices over the intercom. Being the rear gunner on a bomber is kind of like being the goalie for a hockey team; it is a job for an individualist. Still, whenever he is on the ground again, Dan craves the kind of human contact that only Mary can provide. She warms him, she soothes him, and she brings him back to life again.

"What size are you?" she asks him now. "Eleven? Twelve?"

He leans his elbows on the counter and winks at her. "You know what size I am."

First Mary giggles, and then she scolds him. "Stop it, Dan. I mean it! Anyone could hear you."

She bends over to unfold a stepstool, and Dan says, "Mmm, Mary!"

She wags a finger at him. "Stop it, you!"

"Quite contrary," he teases.

Mary tugs a pair of standard-issue, slip-on, fur-lined flying boots from the highest shelf, then steps down and strides over to Dan, slapping them down on the countertop.

"Try these on for size," she says.

"How about a pair of those lace-up officer's boots instead?" he says. "Won't I look dashing in a pair of those?"

"You're already dashing enough, Dapper Dan," she says. "If you were any more handsome, I don't think I could resist you."

Dan puts on a hurt expression. "You mean you can resist me?"

"Shh! Anyone could come in at any time. A superior officer, for example —"

"Come on, Mary! You can spare a pair of those lace-up boots for me, can't you? Every man on the base wants a pair."

Every man on the base wants Mary, too. Dan knows how lucky he is to have somehow won her favour. He wants the boots for a good reason: when he gets back from tomorrow night's raid, Dapper Dan is going to propose to Mary, and he wants to look as absolutely dapper as possible when he does it.

Her suddenly serious expression is amplified by her marble-sculpture cheekbones. "I know that it's cold inside your turret up there," she says. "I've heard of other men freezing their toes off when their heated slippers stopped working. I don't want that to happen to you."

"Aw, Mary," Dan says, "There's no heat in the seat of my suit, and I haven't frozen my ass off yet, so I think my toes will be okay, too. Besides, you know I'm warm-blooded."

He means for this to get a smile out of her, but Mary remains serious. "I want you to be safe up there, Dapper Dan." She reaches across the counter to touch his face. "Every time you cross the Channel, I just about die worrying about you. I want you to come back to me in one piece. Toes and all. Agreed?"

Dan shrugs and takes the fur-lined boots. "Agreed."

The playful sparkle returns to her cornflower-blue eyes, and she says, "If you decide that you don't like them, come back and see me tonight, and maybe I'll give you a pair that you'll like better." She thrusts her chest forward, and her dark eyebrows arch upward in the middle. "I think you'll be satisfied, though. Warm and tight. You can slide right in."

Later that night, while the rest of the personnel at the base are sipping whiskey and playing cards and otherwise distracting themselves from (or fortifying themselves against) tomorrow night's big mission, Dan will indeed pay Mary a visit in the darkened aisles of the supply depot.

Wrapped in the flickering glow of emergency candles and the scratchy warmth of the wool blankets that Mary has "borrowed" from the supply shelves, Mary's nipples will press into the warm flesh of Dan's palms, and her slim fingers will roll the military-issue condom onto Dapper Dan's ample appendage.

Mary will giggle as Dan quotes the slogan from a film he had to watch during training: *"Don't forget! Put it on before you put it in!"*

But then everything will become serious again as Dan presses into the warmth of Mary's body, again and again and again, life and death and life and death and life, again again again.

He will destroy her and he will heal her with every stroke, and she will absorb him and rebirth him over and over and over.

He will need this contact and this release, and so will she. It will help them both to survive another day.

After the emergency candles have burned out, Mary will hold Dan's face and whisper, "Stay alive for me, Daniel."

Mary is the only person who ever calls him Daniel.

Daniel will pull Mary closer to him, and he will whisper in her ear, "You're a good reason to stay alive."

"Gawd-damned old pervert," Nurse Sheila shrieks in her air-raid-siren voice, as she spins Dan away from his view of Clementine's receding backside and shoves his wheelchair into the bathing room. *"You gawd-damned men are all the same. Drooling over these little hussies! Sluts like her are a dime a dozen, mister."*

She strips him like a prisoner of war and then shoves him onto the plastic seat inside the geriatric tub, slamming the door closed and turning the taps on.

"A little warmer, please," Dan says. "I don't like cold water."

"Good gawd," Sheila croaks, *"the water's fine! You're not the only dirty old man I've got to wash today, you know. This isn't a luxury hotel. This isn't a spa."*

"I don't like cold water," Dan repeats.

"You'll live," Sheila barks.

As she slathers his face with liquid soap, Dan drifts backward once again.

This mission is going to be a long, high, cold one, mostly over water, so one of the ground crew smears Dan's face with an extra-thick layer of antifreeze ointment. This is fine with him; he doesn't want his skin to be cracked and chafed from frostbite when he sees Mary tomorrow.

Usually, Dan is inclined to leave a few pieces of gear and clothing behind to give himself a bit more room to move in the tail turret, but Mary's voice has been echoing in his head since last night, saying, *"I want you to be safe up there, Dapper Dan."* So today he wears it all: the silk stockings, the woolen kneecaps, the thermal underwear with the long sleeves and high neck, his combat uniform shirt and pants, the thick white sweater and battledress top, the electrically heated inner suit, the kapok-filled outers. And even though it restricts his movement and makes him feel like a stuffed seal, Dan is even wearing his Mae West life jacket; they'll be flying in high over open water to attack a naval facility, and, if there's a bailout, Dan isn't the best swimmer in the world.

He pulls his new fur-lined flying boots on overtop his heated slippers. There is nothing stylish about these boots, but they will keep his feet warm. A tight-lipped grin spreads across his face as he thinks of Mary saying, *"Warm and tight-fitting. You can slide right in."*

He pushes his fingers into his white silk gloves, then the heated inner gloves, and then the leather gauntlets. *Mary*, he rehearses, *would you do me the honour of…*

His crew hasn't been assigned to one of the new Lancasters after all, so there will be no roomy new Rose turret for Dapper Dan Springthorpe. The bird they're flying is a battered old beast, with sheet-metal patches riveted all over the fuselage like Band-Aids over the bullet holes, and a few gleaming new parts affixed where the old ones were blasted off.

Dan makes his way through the fuselage, through the armoured door at the rear of the plane, and he crams his extra-padded body into the tail gunner's turret. He considers leaving Mae West on the other side of the blast door with his parachute, but then he hears Mary's voice once again: *"I want you to be safe up there, Dapper Dan."*

The Tail End Charlie who occupied the turret before him has already cut away all of the Perspex and armour from between the guns, which has to be done if you actually want to see whatever you're shooting at during a night mission. This previous gunner must have survived his tour, because he's scratched a message into the metal seat: 30 Flights — STILL ALIVE.

Dan has a good feeling about flying in a plane that has survived a lot of missions; this Lancaster is a survivor, just like most of Dan's crew. Sure, there was that eighteen-year-old bomb-aimer who got a stray bullet in the jugular vein when that rocket hit the belly of the Lancaster and exploded a box of ammunition; there was the craggy-faced veteran bombardier (an "old man" of thirty-one) who dropped dead from a heart attack minutes after releasing the last blockbuster on that dam-busting mission; but the other five men on the crew are nearly home free. This mission is their thirtieth.

After thirty flights, you have served your country sufficiently, and your tour of duty is officially over. You can head back home if you want to (although there will be some pressure to stay on and "see the job through"). None of the boys on the crew have mentioned it today, though; nobody wants to jinx this flight.

As soon as his boots touch the runway again tomorrow morning, Dan Springthorpe will sprint to the supply depot, where he will drop to his knees before Mary. The next thing he will do is book two tickets on the first boat back to Canada.

The four V12 Rolls Merlin engines roar to life, and the patched-up old Lancaster shudders up into the air, thirty-six thousand pounds of aircraft, eighteen hundred gallons of fuel, and twelve thousand pounds of bombs straining against the tug of gravity.

Dan takes the message scratched on the seat beneath him as a positive omen: 30 Flights — STILL ALIVE.

This is your lucky day, Daniel Springthorpe, he tells himself. *Nobody is taking your bird down today.*

"Good gawd, man!" Nurse Sheila rages. *"Have you gone even more deaf, or are you just ignoring me? I'm not going to ask you again. Lift your gawd-damned arms!"*

Dan looks at her and says, "Nobody is taking this bird down today."

"Good gawd," Sheila grunts, gripping his thin left arm in one of her meaty paws. *"You're losing your mind, and you're taking mine with you!"*

She wrenches one of Dan's thin limbs upward and then scrubs under his armpit with a sponge as if she's trying to scour rust from old steel.

"Ow! Ow! That hurts!" Dan cries.

"Oh, my gawd! Are you a man or a little crybaby?"

"The water's too deep! It's too cold! You're hurting my arm!"

"Suck it up. Be tough. Believe me, I want to get this over with as much as you do."

Searchlights slash the sky. Luftwaffe night fighters swarm around the Lancaster like bloodthirsty mosquitoes.

"Oh! Oh! It hurts!"

The words buzzing through the intercom belong to the navigator. A Messerschmitt Bf 109 has just hit the belly of the Lancaster with machine-gun fire, and one of the bullets has torn through the navvy's thigh. The top gunner shoots down the 109 a moment later, but this news isn't easing the navigator's pain, nor stopping his blood from gushing out of his body.

Dan Springthorpe squeezes the grips that control the Browning three-oh-threes, and he scans for incoming German fighters, while repeating to himself, "Thirty flights, still alive. Thirty flights, still alive."

The pilot has pushed the Lancaster all the way up to twenty-five-thousand feet, above the anti-aircraft fire, and the veteran bird is shuddering from the stress of the climb. The sky behind the bomber is thick with smoke and debris, backlit by exploding shells and flashing cannon fire. Just below the tail of the Lancaster, Dan watches Halifaxes and Stirlings bursting into flames and disintegrating in the cloud of flak.

The Merlin engines are screaming as the pilot races away from the flashing chaos in the air behind them, and the burning naval yard beneath them.

A sudden jolt rips through the body of the Lancaster.

Dan's skull slams against the back of the turret as the tail whips upward; the nose of the plane is pointed down. The pressure of the sudden dive makes his brain feel like it's going to explode; they are falling *fast*.

Panicked voices hiss through the intercom: "Pull up! Pull up!"

Dan repeats to himself, "Thirty flights, still alive. Thirty flights, still alive."

And then, there is a metallic groan. A convulsion ripples through the fuselage, and the Lancaster levels. Somehow, the pilot has managed to pull the injured bird out of its suicide dive.

"Starboard engines are burning!" another voice crackles through the intercom. "Feather engines! Feather engines!"

Flames flash past Dan's turret. Strips of metal skin peel from the Lancaster's tail fins, revealing the framework underneath.

"Thirty flights, still alive. Thirty flights, still alive."

The Lancaster trembles as more bullets pummel its skin.

"Where the hell *are* you bastards?" Dan hollers. He desperately searches for the attackers, but he can't see them anywhere; they must be above, below, or beside them. The mid-upper gunner will have to get 'em, if he is still alive.

There is another rattle of machine-gun fire, and the bubble window beside Dan explodes. A sharp, burning sensation cuts into his right arm. Blinded by the Perspex dust in his eyes, he feels around for the electrical cords and disconnects his heating suit before he is electrocuted. He accidentally disconnects his oxygen supply, too, but he cannot see to reconnect it properly.

"Abandon aircraft!" comes the command through the intercom. "Bail out, boys! Bail out! Bail —"

The intercom speaker screeches and dies.

As if the blindness isn't bad enough, Dan is becoming woozy and disoriented from oxygen deprivation. He manages to reach behind him, and he levers open the armoured door. He rips off his layers of gloves to more easily feel for his parachute.

After seconds that feel like eternity, Dan's fingers feel it, grab at it greedily, and he manages to snap the parachute onto his harness.

Hopefully it hasn't been damaged in the attack. Hopefully it will open when he needs it to.

Now Dan feels for the controls to rotate his turret to one side so his escape hatch will be facing outward.

Nothing happens. The hydraulic system is damaged. The turret will not rotate.

The tail of the burning Lancaster pitches upward again, and the two remaining live engines scream against the fall.

Broken plastic and twisted metal slash at Dan's bare hands as he gropes for a hole in the turret big enough to pull himself through. His muscles strain against the force of the crippled bomber falling, but somehow he manages to wriggle his shoulders and hips through the jagged hole in the smashed turret.

And then his foot catches on something inside; he is still blind, he can't see what's holding him, but it feels like a cold metal hand is clutching his ankle. It's probably a cable or cord wrapped around his foot.

The engines shriek as the bomber plummets.

Dan twists and pulls and tugs, but whatever is holding him will not let go. If he had a pistol in his hand right now, he would blast off his own foot just to free himself from the doomed aircraft.

"I guess this is it," he says to himself.

Then, as he relaxes his toes, his foot slips free from inside the fur-lined boot. It slides right out.

As Dan spirals through the air, it feels for a moment like he is flying free rather than falling fast.

The wind batters his face, and tears stream from his eyes. Everything is dark and blurry, but he can see again. He can see.

He hears Mary's voice again — "*Stay alive for me, Daniel*" — which reminds him to tug on the rip cord.

He is grateful when the parachute blossoms open overhead.

He sees the ring of flames as the Lancaster crashes into the black water below.

He flutters downward, acutely aware that he isn't dead; he feels the blood pumping through the arteries in his wrists, where he clings to the parachute straps.

He sinks feet first into the cold, churning waves.

He releases his connection to the parachute so it can't drag him under the water.

He hopes that the rest of the crew managed to bail out in time.

He imagines that somehow his mates are still alive.

A wave of cold water washes over him, but also a wave of gratitude.

He feels grateful that Mary insisted on those fur-lined boots, instead of letting him take those fashionable leather lace-ups.

He feels grateful for the Mae West life jacket, which he hugs against him like a lover, like a saviour.

He is overwhelmed with gratitude.

And then he is overcome by the cold. He is shivering, almost convulsing. His teeth chatter against each other with such force he's afraid they might shatter. He thrashes and kicks against the biting cold.

And as the dark, surging waves batter his body, slap his face, and fill his lungs with stinging salt water, he raises his uninjured arm in the air and hollers defiantly, "Thirty flights, still alive! Thirty flights, still alive!"

As Nurse Sheila wrenches his other arm upward, Dapper Dan sings out, "Thirty flights, still alive! Thirty flights, still alive!"

"*You know, mister,*" she says, with a nails-across-a-chalkboard screech, "*you are one crazy old man. You are just freakin' batshit crazy.*"

"Please," Dan pleads, "this water is so cold! Please!"

"*Oh, stop your whining. We'll be done soon.*"

As the water drains out of the geriatric tub, a shaking, chattering Dan climbs out and wraps himself in a towel, feeling quite the opposite of dapper.

"See?" Nurse Sheila huffs. *"It's over now. You lived."*

It's Sunday, and Clementine has taken an extra shift at the home; usually Nurse Sheila claims all of the Sunday shifts for herself because they pay double time, but Sheila has been called away at the last minute. The rumour circulating among the other nurses is that, after all this time, the police have finally found Sheila's late husband's missing hand, and Sheila has been called in to identify and claim the ring that remained upon one mummified finger.

With Sheila absent, Clementine feels a bit more at ease. She wanders out onto the verandah of the veterans' wing, where Dan is parked in his wheelchair. Beside him stands a tall, lean-bodied man with dark hair and eyes. He is wearing a windbreaker with a crest on the chest that reads FAIREVILLE MEMORIAL ARENA; the words ARENA MANAGER are embossed on one sleeve. He appears to be about Clementine's age.

"Aaron," Dan says, in that rumbling, sage-like voice of his, "here comes the young lady that I've been dying for you to meet."

Aaron extends his hand. "You must be Clementine. Great-Gramps here talks about you all the time."

As Clementine takes Aaron's hand, a little jolt of electricity skips through her fingertips and spreads over her skin. She sees the pupils dilate slightly in Aaron's dark eyes, and she wonders if he felt it, too.

"All good things, I hope," Clementine says.

"All good things, believe me," Aaron says. His voice sounds the way that Clementine imagines Dapper Dan's did seventy years ago. "He thinks you're the reincarnation of the woman he was crazy about during the war."

"That's not exactly how I explained it," Dan protests. "I never said 'reincarnation.' You know I don't believe in that stuff. You live, you die, you're gone; that's it, that's all, that's everything."

He shakes his head and shifts in his chair; this is as agitated as Clementine has ever seen him.

"Besides, Mary could still be alive, for all I know. I tried to find her after they let me go, but there are a lot of Mary Browns in the world. She probably has a different name now, anyway. She probably married someone else before they even discharged me." He shrugs his shoulders and sighs. "I suppose she could have found *me*, though, if she'd really wanted to. There aren't so many of us Dan Springthorpes around."

Aaron and Clementine look at each other. Neither is sure what to say.

"But never mind any of that," Dan says, his voice returning to its usual steady tone. "If there are two young people in the world who should meet each other, it's the two of you. Clementine, some folks say that Aaron here is the spitting image of me as a younger man."

"I see the resemblance," she says, unable to pull her gaze away from Aaron.

Aaron cannot look away from Clementine, either.

What is going on here? they both wonder. *Is this what déjà vu feels like?*

"It's kind of incredible that we've never bumped into each other before," Aaron says.

"You only come on Sundays," Dan says to Aaron.

"Sunday is my only day off from work."

"Mine, too," Clementine says. "The one day you come here is the one day that I don't. Fate has been working against us, hasn't it?"

Why did I say that last part? Clementine wonders.

"Well," Dan says, "fate is about to turn in the opposite direction." He shakes a handful of twenty-dollar bills in the air. "Tonight the two of you are going to go out on a date. My treat."

"Oh, Mr. Springthorpe," Clementine says. She never calls him Mr. Springthorpe, but she somehow feels like she should right now. "I can't take your money, and I don't think I can go out on a date with your great-grandson, either. Nurse Sheila would definitely see that as a conflict of interest."

Dapper Dan rolls his eyes. "Well, what Nurse Sheila doesn't know won't hurt her. Or you. And, conflict of interest or not, I see that you two are still holding hands."

Aaron and Clementine both glance downward. It's true.

As their fingers release, Clementine's fingers touch Aaron's wrist, right where the radial artery runs through, and electricity surges through both of their bodies from that tiny point of contact.

It isn't like electrocution, though. It isn't the kind of electricity that hurts or kills. It is stored energy being released, potential energy turning kinetic. It is the kind of electricity that brings people back to life again.

"I don't suppose it would be the end of the world if we shared a meal together," Clementine concedes.

Tomorrow Clementine will return to the Faireville Nursing Home, to empty dirty bedpans, to change colostomy bags, to spoon-feed the frail, to help the fragile out of their beds and into their chairs, to listen to Nurse Sheila call her "Clem" and issue screeching commands. And during her rounds tomorrow, Clementine will find Dapper Dan, his final mission completed, his tour of duty finished.

Tomorrow, Aaron will return to his job at the Faireville Memorial Arena, to change the oil in the Zamboni, to mow the grass around the building, to pick up the trash that's blown onto the parking lot from the high school next door, and to listen to the mayor of Faireville rant over the phone about how the arena "has got to cut its operating budget by twenty percent, or there'll be hell to pay." And then the next phone call he takes will be from Clementine.

In the final moments of today, though, a happily inebriated Clementine will lie back on the rug in Aaron's small living room, and she will convulse with the electricity that surges into her body from Aaron's hands and mouth. And then, on the sofa, her hands and mouth will return every favour, delightful shock by delightful shock.

And then, on top of his bed, Aaron will fill Clementine with his grandfather's inheritance, fully and completely, again and again and again. And again atop the kitchen table. And again on the sofa. And again on the rug. And once more on the bed.

And when the explosions from the final run have burned down to embers, Aaron will say to Clementine, "I feel reborn."

"Or maybe reincarnated," Clementine will reply.

One of Clementine's nipples will press into the pulse in Aaron's wrist as he reaches to slide his finger into the silver ring nestled between Clementine's breasts, which hangs beside her crucifix on a simple, slender chain.

"I had a ring like this once," he says. "It had the same inscription inside, too."

"I thought it was one-of-a-kind," Clementine says.

"I thought that mine was, too."

Just before they fall asleep together, Aaron will whisper, "That was the most perfect day I've had in a very long time."

To which Clementine will reply, "You know, Aaron, you can count the number of perfect days in a year on the toes of one foot."

JAMES YEO IS GOING AWAY

James is jolted awake by his cellphone, which blares its tinny ring tone version of Queen's "We Are the Champions." It takes a moment for James to remember where he is.

The first orange sunlight of the day trickles into the waiting area of Pearson International Airport, Terminal One. Attendants gradually appear behind the airline ticket counters. There is the whirr of wheeled luggage and the hum of hushed conversations as the first passengers of the day move through the airport.

James sits up; there is a pain in his neck where it was pitched over the back of the blue-on-chrome chair. The computer is warm atop his lap; the last words he typed are still backlit on the screen:

> James Yeo is going away.

"We Are the Champions" continues playing.

James hears Roland Baron's voice grunting out the tune, and the endless-loop film of Roland thrusting into Sidney replays on his mental viewscreen, over and over and over again. It makes James's stiff neck itchy and hot. He tugs his leather jacket from the seat beside him and grabs the phone from the inside pocket like he's trying to suffocate it.

"Shut up!" he says, and he punches the answer button, just to make the song stop playing.

"Jimmy Yeo!" Harry Riskey's voice crackles from the cellphone speaker. "Where in THE HELL are you? Have you lost your fucking mind? What in THE HELL has gotten into you?"

James just breathes into the phone.

Harry screams again, with evangelical furor, "What in THE HELLLLLLLLLL has gotten INTO YOU?"

James stares out into the white blur of the airport and says evenly, "Maybe you should ask Sidney what's gotten into her."

"The cops tried to contact Sidney after they found the car, James. When they couldn't find her, they came to me, James. What in THE HELL were you thinking? What in THE HELL is the matter with you?"

Oh. Right. The car. James had forgotten about the car.

After his visit to Priya's place, James stopped for a few drinks at a local bar. Well, more than just a few. He may have blacked out at some point. When he came to, the interior of the Honda Civic was clouded with powder from the airbag deploying. Through the cracked windshield, a slim suburban maple tree seemed to be growing out from under the crumpled hood.

James had to ram the door with his shoulder a few times to force it open, as the impact had wedged it slightly into the door frame. Then he casually stepped out of the smashed Civic. The car was crumpled, but he was relatively undamaged. He felt fine. Physically, anyway.

Out of habit, James grabbed his briefcase from the passenger seat and then strolled to the nearest main street, where he hailed the first taxi he saw.

And now here he is. YYZ. The song starts playing in his head again, thankfully drowning out "We Are the Champions." But then Harry Riskey's voice continues raging through the cellphone speaker: "I do NOT appreciate having my home visited by cops in the middle of the night, Jimmy! That is NOT what I need."

"Did you think it was a fraud investigation, Harry?"

"What? What did you say? What do you think you know about ..."

Harry pauses. James can picture him pacing back and forth across the endangered-species hardwood floor of his den.

"Jimmy," Harry says, now doing his best imitation of fatherly, "what happened? Why did you abandon the car like that?" His voice becomes almost angelic. "Is there something upsetting you, Jimmy? Did something happen at the doctor's office? You can talk to me, Jimmy. I'm here for you, Jimmy."

On the rare occasion that Harry makes a sales call, he is prone to repeating the target's name over and over like this. James knows the technique too well.

"It's *James*, Harry. Not Jimmy. My name is *James*."

"Talk to me, James," he says, practically purring. "I'm here for you, James."

"Harry," James says, pausing for some time. He wants to phrase this in just the right way. "I don't think that Sidney and I are going to be providing you with any heirs."

"Awwwww, I knew it!" Harry bawls. "I knew you were shooting blanks! I knew it was you! I knew it wasn't Sidney!"

"No," James says, "it's because of Sidney."

"How could it possibly be her fault? It couldn't possibly be her fault."

"Harry," James says, pausing just for effect this time, "your daughter ..."

He pauses again. The suspense must be killing Harry. *Killing Harry* ... James smiles at this.

"Your daughter," James repeats, "is an adulteress."

"What? What? WHAT?" Harry yelps. "What did you just call my little girl?"

James could have said "slut" or "whore," but he almost never uses words like that, even under extreme duress. James just isn't that kind of guy.

Harry sputters, "My Sidney would never … she would never!"

"Well, Harry," James says, "your Sidney *did*. In *our* house. In *our* bed. In our *bed*, Harry. And in the kitchen, too. When I left, they were going at it on the balcony."

There is a silence before the explosion.

"Th-then it's YOUR OWN F-F-FAULT, you f-f-fucking u-u-useless, b-blank-shooting F-F-FUCKHEAD!"

Harry is stuttering. This means that he is really, *really* pissed off. James has seen it before at the office. Harry's bald dome will be glowing like a supernova. His clenched fists will be shaking like little earthquakes.

"Sh-she p-probably j-just wanted to be with a R-REAL M-MAN for a f-fucking change! One who is c-capable of getting her F-F-F-FUCKING P-PREGNANT!"

Normally, James cowers under Harry's stormy tantrums, winces against his wind. But not this time. The more Harry rages, the calmer James feels. He feels as if he might float away, just drift up into the heavenly white space of Pearson International Airport.

"Ya don't have anything to f-fucking say to THAT, do ya, ya useless little F-FAGGOT?" Harry roars. "Ya don't have anything to say to THAT, D-DO YA?"

"Harry," James says, feeling even lighter as he inhales, "they were using condoms. Lots of them. *Ribbed for her pleasure,* Harry. *With spermicidal lubricant.*"

For maybe the first time ever, Harry Riskey is speechless.

"Goodbye, Harry," James says.

When "We Are the Champions" blares again, James switches the phone off. He drops it into a nearby garbage receptacle and then floats back to his seat, humming the tune of "YYZ."

He has to type with both hands. He doesn't have any time to waste.

He logs on to the Riskey and Gamble corporate website.

And then his LinkedIn page.

And then his Twitter account.

And then his Facebook page.

And then his Gmail account.

Eighteen quick keystrokes each. Four little words.

And then he pushes the power button.

The screen goes blank, and the laptop's hard drive and cooling fan whirl to silence. James closes the computer, property of Riskey and Gamble, and carries it over and drops it into the same garbage container as the cellphone. After removing his passport, he tosses in the briefcase, too.

Then he twists the silver ring on his finger — *clockwise, counter-clockwise, clockwise, counter-clockwise* — but it resists. It doesn't want to come off. So James will wear it for now, and decide what to do with it six weeks from now.

His mental soundtrack thunders "YYZ" as he strides toward the ticket desk.

"You're lucky," the attendant says. "There were a lot of last-minute cancellations, so there are seats available on just about every flight. That was some crazy weather yesterday, eh?"

"Record breaking," James says.

The passenger in the seat beside him is a young woman with a wistful look on her face. There is the usual pre-flight small talk.

"Business or pleasure?" she asks.

"Escape," James says. "Or maybe adventure."

"Me too, I think," she says. "How long are you travelling for?"

"Six weeks," James says, "or possibly less. But hopefully more."

"Same here, more or less," she says. "I'm going to travel until I run out of money."

"I'm going to travel until I run out of time."

"My name is Emily."

"I'm James. James Yeo."

"Well, James Yeo," Emily says, "here's to new beginnings."

James will be looking out the airplane window, watching Toronto disappear beneath him, before anyone reads his final message to them all:

James Yeo is gone.

CORONATION

As the Queen emerges from the alley behind the dry cleaner's shop on Dundas Street, a small child collides with her borrowed Loblaw's shopping cart. The little girl stumbles backward, her eyes wide.

The Queen asks in her gravelly voice, "Did you get away from your momma, little one?" The child drops her chocolate-glazed doughnut on the sidewalk; it leaves a brown streak down the front of her pink, officially licensed Disney Princess Jasmine sweatshirt. She fixates on the scar that cuts diagonally through the Queen's upper and lower lip. She takes another step backward and takes in the large woman's yellowish skin, her matted, Medusa-like hair, her dark stubbly moustache, her chipped, clawlike fingernails. Five years of watching Disney Princess movies has taught her that old women who look like this one are witches. *Evil* witches.

The Queen smiles at the moppet and extends her hand. The child interprets the baring of her sporadic yellow-brown teeth as a threatening snarl, and the intrusion of the Queen's gnarled, claw-nailed fingers as an attempt to kidnap her. Kidnapping precious little girls is what evil witches do.

The child opens her mouth wide, pitches back her head, and shrieks, "MOMMY! MOMMY! MOMMY!"

Her mother races around the corner, clip-clopping like an injured racehorse atop stiletto heels. She pauses to drop her state-of-the-art smartphone into her oversized purse (which is festooned with big brass tags advertising the brand name), and then she wails, "You stay away from my baby, you bitch! You stay away from my baby!"

The child bursts into tears as her mother tugs her away from the Queen. "Bitch" sounds so much like "witch"! Mommy has just proved that evil witches exist in the real world, outside the safety of Disney Animated Classics™.

"Did she touch you, Amberlindzy?" her mother frets. "Did she touch you, precious?"

As they rush toward the safe haven of an upscale shoe store, the fashionable mother frantically digs inside her purse for a bottle of Safety First!™ antibacterial hand sanitizer (with Aloe Vera), to protect her offspring from whatever vile venom the Queen may have transmitted to her.

With a grunt, the Queen bends over to pick up the chocolate-glazed doughnut from the sidewalk.

Everyone needs to eat.

Brandy Foley is wearing a shimmering imported kimono, which she has allowed to fall open to reveal the deep valley between her Malibu Barbie breasts. She admires her reflection in the glass case that displays her Miss Theodore Buttermilk Festival Pageant crown.

A few weeks ago, Brandy removed the sash from the case and took it to a dry cleaner on Dundas Street that specializes in cleaning fine gold lamé, and who also claimed to have the "Best Seamstress in Toronto" working on site. In red silk letters, the words BUTTERMILK FESTIVAL BEUTY QUEEN had been sewn onto the sash, and although Brandy had folded it inside the case to conceal this imperfection, the Beuty Queen had decided that it was finally time to have the error corrected.

Now Brandy opens the case again, and she gingerly plucks the red-rhinestone-encrusted, gold-electroplated tiara from the prongs that hold it in place. She nestles it atop her hair, which is salon-perfect, despite Brandy having just crawled out of bed. She turns around and glides through the foyer, her crown sailing through the air like a ruby yacht atop gentle waves. She allows her surgically enhanced breasts to spring free from the confines of her robe; they bob before her like hanging tetherballs, or emergency floatation devices.

"Mom," Tiffany says, "what are you doing?"

Brandy Foley pulls the kimono closed over her chest, tugs the crown from her hair, and says, "Well, um, since I'm having my pageant sash refreshed, I thought maybe my tiara could use a little recharge, too. There's a jewellery store downtown that specializes in ultrasound-polishing large items like crowns. Want to come with me, sweetie?"

"Um, well ..."

"We can go out somewhere nice for lunch."

Tiffany's stomach rumbles and gurgles; although there are nearly three hundred bottles of wine stored in the climate-controlled basement cellar, there is rarely any food in the walk-in refrigerator, since Mr. Foley is rarely ever home, and Mrs. Foley rarely ever eats.

Tiffany Foley shrugs. "Okay, I guess. Can we eat *before* we go to the jeweller?"

Everyone needs to eat.

Tiffany is so hungry now, she feels like she might faint.

Her mother took almost an hour to cram her amplified curves into a satiny minidress, which likely cost more than the maid's monthly income. Then she took nearly another hour to "put on her face" and "accessorize."

Tiffany, on the other hand, was ready to go in five minutes: two minutes and a dozen bobby pins to do her hair up like a Motown backup singer, and three minutes to pull on the vintage sixties dress she picked up at the Goodwill store downtown, the Wonder Woman bracelets from Chinatown, and the sheer smoky nylons from a discount store in Kensington Market.

Tiffany's friend Abby showed her the hairdo trick, and where to find cheap used clothing. Abby is one of the few girls at Ladycrest who is there on a scholarship (to raise the school's official academic average, Tiffany theorizes). Tiffany's entire outfit cost less than forty dollars, and this makes her feel proud of herself. Abby is right; Tiffany could survive without her father's money if she had to.

Now Tiffany and her mother are sitting on the patio at Trattoria Mercatto, a sit-down, table-service restaurant adjoined to the Eaton Centre mall. Tiffany would have been happy to just devour a Taco Bell burrito to satisfy her hunger, but her mother just rolled her eyes and gasped, "The *food court*, Tiffany? Did I raise you in a *barn*?"

Brandy Foley has decided that this place will do, since they aren't anywhere near Scaramouche or Sotto Sotto. The well-groomed planters around the patio show that they are at least *trying* to be civilized here, and the natural sunlight is a small bonus; it will add some tone to Brandy's heat lamp–bronzed skin.

Tiffany looks up at the canvas awning that hangs above the restaurant's windows. Its valance is printed with the words INSALATE, ZUPPA, ANTIPASTI, PIZZE, VINI; if it had simply read "Salads, Soup, Appetizers, Pizzas, and Wines," her mother certainly would have turned her nose up at this place, too.

"Sorry for the wait, ladies," the harried server says as she arrives with menus. She is not much older than Tiffany. "It's so busy here today!"

Brandy wheezes, "I guess they should hire more servers, then, shouldn't they?"

"It's okay," Tiffany says apologetically. "We weren't waiting long."

Her brain feels like it's eating itself, and she can't get her eyes to focus on the fine print on the menu, so Tiffany just orders the first thing she recognizes without reading the description underneath. "I'll have the pepperoni pizza," she says.

"Hmm ..." Brandy says, taking a long, deep breath. "I'm wavering between the scallops and the calamari ... but tell me, is your seafood flown in fresh, or is it previously frozen?"

"I'm pretty sure it's fresh."

"Are the scallops *bay* scallops or *sea* scallops?"

"They're the big ones. Sea scallops. Bay scallops are the little ones they put in the pasta."

"Are they seared or grilled?"

"I'm sure I can have them prepared either way, ma'am."

As her mother interrogates the server as if she's negotiating the Treaty of Versailles, Tiffany's gaze wanders across the square to the Church of the Holy Trinity. It's where the Cowboy Junkies recorded their album *The Trinity Session*. Abby played it for her the last time that Tiffany slept over. Abby's parents' apartment is small, but they've got an incredible vinyl collection.

A Cowboy Junkies song is playing in her head now, and Tiffany thinks to herself, *I've been to the Eaton Centre a hundred times, and I've never poked my head inside Holy Trinity. Maybe today I will.*

She's brought back to the patio of Trattoria Mercatto by her mother's continuing interrogation of the server.

"Are the scallops breaded?

"No, ma'am. They're fresh, brushed with a touch of garlic butter."

"Could you have the chef use extra-light virgin olive oil instead? Or, even better, fine-filtered almond oil, if you've got it."

"I can ask."

"Oh, and one more thing. Are they Atlantic or Pacific scallops?"

"Um … Atlantic? I think the distributor is based in Newfoundland."

"Wild or farmed?"

"Well, um, wild, I suppose, if they're from the Atlantic Ocean."

"Hmm …" Brandy says, knitting her brows as if she's contemplating theorems of fractal relativity. "You know what? I prefer *Mediterranean* scallops. So I think I'll just have the *misticanza*."

Tiffany resists rolling her eyes when her mother pronounces *misticanza* with an exotic-sounding invented accent. She's pretty sure that in Italian, *misticanza* just means "house salad."

The server is halfway to the kitchen inside, when Brandy calls out after her, "Miss! Miss!"

The saintly, patient young woman weaves her way through the crowded restaurant back to their table.

"You know what? I'd like a glass of champagne as well."

"Well, it's an Italian restaurant, ma'am, so we've got Prosecco, not champagne."

Brandy sighs and blinks her eyes. "That will have to do, I suppose."

She waits until the server is back inside the building again before crying out, "And no tomatoes on my salad! I'm *very allergic* to tomatoes!"

Tiffany shakes her head. Her mother is *not* allergic to tomatoes; Brandy read on some scientifically dubious weight-loss website that tomatoes cause post-menopausal women to retain water, so now she has to avoid them *at all costs*!

Brandy's phone rings. "Hello-ooo!" she sings into it. "Brandy Foley speaking.… Oh, yes … is my sash cleaned already? Oh, good, I'll pop over and … *what*?" Her eyes bug out as if they're going to pop. Thanks to the Botox paralysis, though, her eyebrows and forehead remain eerily unanimated. "You have got to be kidding me. You have got to be fucking *kidding* me!"

She's screaming now. People are glaring at her. Tiffany wants to crawl under the patio table and hide.

"I will be at your shop in one hour," Brandy rages into the phone, "and you had better find it by then, or there will be hell to pay. My husband is Stringfellow Foley. He can put you out of business with one phone call. Understood? Good."

Tiffany's mother slams her phone down on the tabletop, rattling the tableware. "Those idiots at the dry cleaners lost my pageant sash. Can you believe it?"

"I'm sure they'll find it," Tiffany says, secretly hoping that they won't.

Their orders arrive quickly; the server must have discerned that Brandy Foley is the *particular* sort. Tiffany immediately devours her pizza, while her mother waits for the server to bring her a replacement fork, since her previous fork was "dirty" in some way visible only to her own blue-tinted eyes.

A rumpled, bearded man crosses Trinity Square and approaches the rails of the patio. He holds out a calloused, sun-leathered hand. Practically whispering, slurring his words as if he's had a stroke, he says, "Ssssspare change for sssome fffood, prrrretty lllladies?"

Maybe it's the hunger-headache that is still ringing inside her skull, or maybe it's the rush of blood from her brain to her stomach to digest the food she's finally eating, but the scolded-dog sadness in this wrinkled man's dark eyes, and the desperation in his hushed, blurred words make Tiffany feel like bursting into tears.

As she leans over to reach into her purse, her mother shrieks, "Shoo! Shoo! Go away! Git! Git!" She waves her hand at him, as if this bent, skeletal man is a raccoon who has just knocked over her garbage can.

"Mom! Gawd! He's just hungry!"

But it is too late. He turns and hobbles away, toward the steps of Holy Trinity.

"Good *gawd*!" Brandy says. "There are *more* of them over there. Is there a bum convention at the church today, or what? I suppose they'll *all* be over here soon, begging for our money instead of going out and earning their own."

Tiffany is about to say, *"When did you start earning your own money, Mother?"* but then the server appears with a new clean fork. Spit-polished, Tiffany hopes.

Brandy turns to the server. "Can't you do something about these" — she pauses. She can't *publicly* call them bums — "these *vagrants* hanging around your patio? They're harassing your customers! What kind of business are you running here, anyway?"

"Well, ma'am, it's a public square, so we can't really control who uses it."

"Their *smell* makes the food unappetizing," Brandy says, wrinkling her nose. "Now bring me another glass of champagne."

"Please," Tiffany adds.

"Another glass of Prosecco right away," the server says, choosing wisely to retreat.

Tiffany gazes over at the tall, grey doors of the church across the square, if only to avoid looking at her mother, by whom she is even more embarrassed than usual.

About two dozen people are now gathered in a scattered semicircle around the church entrance. Some of the people look frayed and scruffy: women with weathered skin and matted, windblown hair, men with downcast eyes and wild wizard beards; people that Tiffany's mother classifies as "bums." Some of the people are dressed in nondescript workday clothes, with sensible haircuts and shoes designed for comfortable walking; people whom Brandy Foley calls "plain Janes."

A tall, slender man dressed in black places a small candle in each person's hand. The candles are topped with little white plastic cups, to prevent their tiny flames from being extinguished by the breeze.

A few people in crisply pressed suits and knee-length, business-district skirts accept the candles tentatively, as if they have accepted the King's shilling and they're about to be shanghaied. They glance around nervously, worried that they will look like jerks if they just continue on into the Eaton Centre food court without pausing to observe whatever solemn affair is going on here.

A woman with a microphone begins reading a list of names: "John Doe, July third … Jane Doe, July seventeenth … Russell 'Red' Brown, July twenty-first … John Doe, July twenty-second … 'Rhymin' Simon Jones, July twenty-ninth …"

Brandy Foley's unamplified voice interrupts, ringing in Tiffany's ears.

"Oh. My. GAWD!" she yelps. "There is a *tomato seed* in my *misticanza*! I told that idiot *specifically* that I am *allergic* to —"

"For gawd's sake, Mom," Tiffany sighs. "It's just a *cucumber* seed. There are *cucumber slices* in your salad."

Brandy Foley shoves her plate away. "Well, I'm not eating it, and I'm not paying for it. And I'm not tipping her, either. Snotty little bitch. Did you hear the attitude she was giving me?"

Tiffany predicts what will happen next. Her mother will pick a fight with the waitress. The management will be summoned. Reparations will be demanded. Stringfellow Foley's name will be mentioned, as if he is some kind of vengeful deity.

Tiffany slides her chair back; it screeches angrily against the patio bricks. "I'm going for a walk. Text me when you've finished getting your crown polished, okay?"

"Don't go giving your money to any of those bums."

"I'll do what I want with my money," Tiffany says. "My allowance isn't as big as yours, but it's still mine."

She stands, turns, and walks through the patio gate and into Trinity Square, toward the rumpled, sad-eyed man, who stands at the edge of the gathered crowd.

Although others are sniffling and wiping away tears, the Queen does not cry when Rhymin' Simon's name is read. When you've got Royal Blood pumping through your veins, you don't cry in public. You can't. It would not be regal behavior.

Her lower lip quivers, though, and she repeats his name in a low, rumbling whisper, "Rhymin' Simon Jones. Rhymin' Simon Jones."

The Queen has acquired some new clothes for the occasion, to show respect for her deceased comrade. She's wearing her usual long beige raincoat, which is pocked with rust-coloured stains from the bridge's drippings, but underneath she's dressed to the nines, as a queen should be when attending a function. She obtained a lovely purple velveteen blouse from the donation box in front of the Sally Ann, and a golden royal sash that called out to her when she peeked through the unlocked back door of that dry cleaner's shop on Dundas.

The sash was destined for the Queen. It was displayed by Providence specifically for her. Its fine gold lamé was meant to be worn by someone with Royal Blood. It even has the word QUEEN sewn onto it in red silk letters. (With her saw blade fingernails, the Queen picked off those other unnecessary letters: BUTTERMILK FESTIVAL BEUTY.)

Simon would have liked her new sash. He once brought her a brooch that someone had tossed into his begging cup. It was a chubby Siamese cat with a faux ruby for a belly. After he handed it to her, he said:

Queen Elizabeth One had a Siamese kitty,
and here is another for the Queen of the City.

The brooch is fastened to the Queen's gold lamé sash now.

The memorial service is over. The church people and the social workers and the hungry file into the Church of the Holy Trinity for the free meal that follows the vigil, to be fed, to be hydrated, and to receive temporary shelter from the heat and bright sunlight. The Holy Trinity, indeed: Food. Water. Shelter.

The politely trapped and the curious passersby hand their cup-topped candles back to the slender man in black, and they head for the revolving glass doors of the Eaton Centre, back to their own realities. Hundreds more flit about inside the urban mall, eating burritos and burgers, buying smartphones and purses and shoes, unaware of the little church just outside.

By the time Tiffany crosses the square, the crowd is dispersing, and the sad-eyed bearded man is already gone. Beside the church steps stands a lopsided, wild-haired woman wearing a stained beige overcoat. She is facing a sign that reads:

TORONTO HOMELESS MEMORIAL
Memorial Service — Second Tuesday of Each
Month at 12 Noon

Tiffany watches the woman reach out to touch the glass case below the sign; her arthritic fingers are gnarled like the twigs of an ancient tree branch, and her long claw-nails are yellowed and cracked. Tiffany moves to stand beside her; she is going to help *somebody* today.

Without looking at Tiffany, the woman says, "His name isn't in there. They ran out of room for new names a while ago."

Tiffany reads the small note tucked into the bottom corner of the case:

> This list includes 700+ names of men, women, and children who have lived and died on the streets of Toronto as a direct result of homelessness. Stop, pause, and remember all of these people and the many more who continue to struggle as they live on our streets. Then call your local city councillor, the mayor, your MPP, and your MP. Help solve the homelessness disaster.

The woman turns and shuffles away across the uneven bricks of Trinity Square, dragging her left foot, listing to one side.

"Ma'am," Tiffany says, "do you need some help?"

The Queen is a lot more stable when she has her borrowed Loblaw's shopping cart to hang on to, but today she has left it behind in her secret hiding place near the bridge. It would be unbecoming to arrive all sweaty and dirty to Simon's memorial service. She came on the subway, entered without a token. "The Queen needs no fare!" she screamed at the sleepy-eyed operator inside the ticket booth. He made no attempt to stop her.

"I'm fine," the Queen says, holding her regal nose high in the air. "I am the Queen, my dear. My chariot will take me to my Rosedale estate."

Tiffany strides up beside her. "I'm going to Rosedale, too. May I assist you, then, my queen?"

Tiffany offers her arm, and the Queen takes it. They move through the mall together and descend into Dundas station; Tiffany somehow understands that the Queen's chariot is the Yonge subway line.

When the Queen unbuttons her size-too-small raincoat to allow herself to sit down inside the subway car, Tiffany sees the gold lamé pageant sash. Her eyes widen. *It couldn't possibly be, could it?*

Then she sees the remnants of red thread, outlining the shape of the words *FESTIVAL BEUTY*.

Oh. My. Gawd.

Tiffany digs her phone out of her purse and immediately types a text to Brandy Foley:

> Hey, Mom. Don't wait for me. Taking the subway home.

A smirk spreads across Tiffany's face. She taps another text to her mother:

> BTW, any luck with the dry cleaners?

* * *

At the abutment of the Rosedale Valley Bridge, the Queen says, "I must leave you now, my dear. The location of my abode is a closely guarded secret." Then she smiles her spacious, yellow-brown smile. "Thank you for your help."

The Queen stands there with her nose in the air, and Tiffany understands that she is being dismissed.

As she turns to walk away, The Queen says, "Wait! What is your name, dear?"

"Tiffany. My name is Tiffany."

"I thought that your name might be Mary. My daughter's name was Mary," says the Queen. "They took her away when the bad things happened."

This is the first time that the Queen has said her daughter's name in a long, long time.

"I'm sorry," Tiffany says.

The Queen reaches inside her speckled beige overcoat, steps toward Tiffany, drops a warm, round object into her hand. It's a sprayed-gold Siamese cat, with a red plastic ruby for a belly.

"The first Queen Elizabeth had a Siamese cat," The Queen says. Then a dark cloud passes over her expression, and she looks away. "You had better go now, dear."

Tiffany takes several dozen steps before looking over her shoulder, to see the Queen hobbling over the edge of the Rosedale Ravine and disappearing beneath the bridge.

Brandy Foley's Cadillac Escalade and Stringfellow Foley's Porsche Cayenne are both parked outside their turreted Victorian mansion.

"Mom! Dad!" Tiffany cheers as she bursts through the front door. "I've decided what I'm going to do to earn my volunteer —"

She is interrupted by her mother, who pushes past her.

Brandy Foley is sobbing hysterically, her face cobwebbed with tear-diluted black mascara. "What do you care, you fucker!" she screams at her husband, who stands just inside the grand entry foyer.

The glass door of Brandy's Beuty Queen display case swings gently on its hinges, and Brandy's ultrasound-polished pageant crown dangles from her fingertips.

She pauses in the doorway and cries, "If you don't care, then I don't care either, you son of a bitch!"

Dramatically, Brandy Foley steps out onto the portico and flings the tiara out onto the immaculately groomed golf-green lawn that surrounds their perfect Rosedale home.

"Come back inside, Brandy," Stringfellow Foley commands. "Do you want someone to see you in this … this *state*?"

"Oh, am I *embarrassing* you, String?" Brandy rages, looking as angry as her Botox-paralyzed facial muscles will allow. "You can't *possibly* be as embarrassed as I was when I found out that you're *fucking your assistant*!"

"My gawd, Brandy," String barks, "we were just having lunch! Everyone has to eat."

"*Somebody's* getting eaten, I'll bet!" Brandy shrieks, spittle exploding from her collagen-plumped lips. "It's the last straw, String! I'm leaving you!"

She storms from the portico. The door slams on the Escalade, and its tires screech as she speeds away.

Stringfellow Foley turns to his daughter. "Apparently I wasn't upset enough about her losing her pageant sash."

Tiffany just stares at him.

"Don't worry, Princess, she'll be back. She couldn't survive for a week on the money she'd get from the pre-nup."

"Dad?" Tiffany says.

"Yes, Princess?"

"Don't call me Princess anymore, okay?"

Tiffany wanders outside, and she sends a text to her friend Abby.

Hey, can I sleep at your place?

Sure. Tonight?

Maybe indefinitely.

As she strides away from the mansion, Tiffany's foot nicks something in the grass. She leans over to pluck her mother's tiara from the turf with her left hand. Then she opens the fingers of her right hand and looks at the red-bellied Siamese cat nestled in the warmth of her palm.

Maybe this is a sign, Tiffany thinks.

The Queen awakes to the sound of tires whirring across the bridge above her. She crawls out from under her tarpaulin and glances up at her borrowed Loblaw's shopping cart, to make sure that nobody has made off with any of her treasures during the night. She is sure that she heard an intruder in the night, but she was too tired and sore to move.

Her eyes widen. Perched atop the cart is what appears to be a tiara. A monarch's crown.

The Queen staggers to her feet and hobbles over to the cart.

It is a crown. Gold, with rubies.

Maybe this is a sign, the Queen thinks.

She plucks the tiara from its place atop her other treasures; she nestles it into her matted hair, and the suppressed memories surge, a rolling wave that the Queen can no longer hold back.

My grandmother was a beautiful woman. She had a queen's name, too: Mary.

The Queen stands a little straighter.

My mother had a queen's name, too. She was called Victoria.

"My name is Elizabeth," she says out loud. "I gave my daughter a queen's name, too: Mary. After my grandmother."

When the bad things happened, they sent Mary to live with some farmers. Nice people, they said. Responsible, decent, church-going people.

When she places the crown back atop her borrowed Loblaw's cart, she notices something else there, something that she didn't see before.

It's a silver ring. She picks it up. There are some words engraved inside: *Forever More.*

What did they rename her? Valencia? Something like that. Something orangey.

The Queen slips the ring onto her swollen, scabbed ring finger, and her eyes widen.

"No," she says. "It was Clementine. They renamed my baby Clementine."

Between the thumb and index finger of her right hand, the Queen twists the simple silver ring. *Clockwise, counter-clockwise. Clockwise, counter-clockwise.*

And then she does something that she has not done in a very, very long time.

The Queen makes a wish.

EFFECT

(EPILOGUE)

STORM

Then, out of nowhere, a storm arrives.

You know that it didn't really come from out of nowhere. It isn't as surprising as that. We're still members of the animal kingdom, we humans. We can still feel storms coming. We just don't pay as close attention as the other beasts do. We have other things on our minds. But in the back of our head, in that little space left over from our savage beginnings, we feel them coming. We know.

There is that lull, that eerie peace, when everything is just a little too quiet, a silence too perfect to ever be anything but temporary. We hear the absence of the wind; we rarely notice anything usual until it disappears.

No birds chirp. No footsteps are heard. There are no blurred conversations from the backyards beyond the parking lot outside.

Silence and stillness slip away, and the prelude begins: a distant tympanic rumble, a sound like a rocket climbing up through the atmosphere.

rrrrrrrrRRRRRRRRRRRRRRrrrrrrrrrrr ...

The sky is a bruise, greyish-purple and soft. Fingers of cloud spread overhead like a wounded hand, then the whole palm cups the sky, obscuring the pinpoint lights of stars.

tick

A single raindrop strikes the glass, an invitation. You rise from your purring-cat position atop the furniture, drawn to the edge of the screen door, where a current of air ruffles the curtain, swirls the silky material like the dress of the belle of the ball.

tick

Maybe you escaped on a train. Perhaps you have just made love to the stranger who sat beside you on your flight out of the country. Perhaps you were never strangers at all.

tick tick

You are perhaps a young woman who has just been contacted by her birth mother. Perhaps you have just made love to celebrate this revelation.

tick

You are perhaps the great-grandson of a man who loved the great-grandmother of your lover. Perhaps in some way they have just made love also.

tick tick

Perhaps you are genetically predestined to want each other. Perhaps that is why you have just made love.

tick tick tick

Maybe you just received a phone call from your doctor's office, informing you that your file was mixed up with another, and that you probably have more than a month to live. Maybe you have just made love to celebrate this revelation.

tick

Maybe you received no call at all. Maybe you still feel like you could die at any moment, and maybe this makes you want to make love as if it's for the very last time.

tick tick

Perhaps you met her atop the tower. Or perhaps neither of you could wait six weeks. Perhaps your own affair to remember is about to begin.

tick tick tick

Maybe you have just given a ring as a gift. Perhaps you have just received one. Maybe the ring is for a woman, not a man. Perhaps it is engraved with the words *For Evermore.*

tick tick tick tick

Perhaps you think, or even say, "We got it right this time."

tick tick tick tick tick ticktickticktick

hissssssSSSSSSS …

An unspoken mutual decision, you step through the screen door, to feel the wind flow against you, your feet bare and tentative upon the cool concrete outside.

The drumroll of thunder begins, builds to a slow crescendo — like a rocket's engines roaring against gravity.

h r r h r r r r r r h r r r r R R R R R R R R-ROOOOOOOOOMMMmmmm …

Do you tremble with delight? Anticipation? Fear? Or is it just the rush of thunder reverberating inside your chest?

Rain assaults the pavement now, crackling, roaring defiance against the horizontal wall of pavement that prevents it from streaking downward forever.

Rain hisses upon the lawn, forcing the blades of grass to bow over, to submit.

Rain roars like a million cheering voices, a frenzied crowd at a rally — a chorus at first, then a ghostly choir, but now a mob-like roar; the sound of a rocket breaking free.

rrrrrrrrCCRACKOOOOOOWWwwwwwwwww

Do your fingers grip a little tighter, increase your stake in this tantrum of nature?

Above it all, chain lightning dances a fragmented streak across the sky, free, alive with energy, immortal.

But only for a fraction of a second. Its pattern is burned red, purple, then blue into your eyes when you blink, a mere afterthought of the free, crazy energy.

The lightning is receding; the next flash is farther away, as is the next flash, and the next, and the flash that follows that. And soon the light is distant, and there is just a gentle, infant sprinkling, a small reminder of what had been.

It is cool now, the air reborn, almost sweet to the lungs.

You still have each other's hands.

And you are not the only ones.

NOTES

The town of Faireville, which serves as the setting for some chapters, is fictional, although some details are borrowed from the author's previous hometowns of Olinda, Leamington, Kingsville, and Petrolia, Ontario.

The city of Toronto, on the other hand, is real (despite occasional arguments to the contrary). However, the author may have slightly reconfigured certain elements of the city to suit his fictional purposes.

There are approximately five thousand homeless people sleeping either outdoors or in emergency shelters on any given night in the city of Toronto. A large number of these people live in the Rosedale Ravine, which borders Rosedale, the wealthiest neighbourhood in the city.

The Church of the Holy Trinity is an Anglican church in downtown Toronto; its slogan is "Loving Justice in the Heart of the City." The church holds an outdoor memorial service on the second Tuesday of every month to remember those who have died without a place to call home.

All of the characters in this book are, in fact, characters, meaning that they are products of the author's imagination. You can find out more about the author and the products of his imagination at www.richardscarsbrook.com.

ACKNOWLEDGEMENTS

"The Final Ring," then called "The Third Ring," was a finalist for the Fish Flash Fiction Prize, and was published, in a rather different form, in *The Fish Anthology* (Fish Publishing, Bantryr, Ireland, 2011).

"Blink" was published in the Spring 2015 issue of *Reed Magazine* (U.S.). It was also shortlisted for the 2014 Seán Ó Faoláin Short Story Prize (Ireland).

"Royal Blood" and "Coronation" were published as a single story called "Royal Blood" in the Winter 2014 issue of *The Nashwaak Review*.

"Half-Life" was published in *The Wild Quarterly*, September 2014.

An early version of "You Deserve Better! You Deserve More!" was published in *Draft 9.6*, the publication of the Draft Reading Series in Toronto, where the story was read for the first time in early 2014.

A longer short story called "Downpour" (consisting of "Moving Is Easier than Renovating," "Property of Riskey and Gamble," "The Receptionist," and "Half-Life") was longlisted for the 2015 Short Fiction Prize.

A very different version of "Storm" was published in *Canadian Writer's Journal*, Fall 1999. A poem version of "Storm" also appeared in the author's poetry collection *Six Weeks* (Turnstone Press, 2013).

A poem version of "Rocks and Rockets," called "Effect," will appear in the author's poetry collection *Apocalypse One Hundred* (Turnstone Press, 2017).

GRATITUDE

For generous support during the creation of this book, my sincere thanks to the Toronto Arts Council, the Ontario Arts Council, and the Canada Council for the Arts.

I worked on portions of this book during my term as Writer in Residence at the North York Central Library (fall 2014). Thank you to Greg Kelner, Muriel Hart, Matthew Dimuantes, and everyone else at the Toronto Public Library for the opportunity to assist the public with their writing projects while also developing my own.

Thanks to everyone at Dundurn, especially my editor, Shannon "the Fiction Guru" Whibbs. I also owe a debt of gratitude (and reciprocal proofreading) to my author friends who gave this book a final read-through before it went to press: Dan Perry, Heather Wood, Ann Ewan, and Valerie Connor.

Thanks as always to my many fun, literate, and loyal friends. To once again paraphrase Bill Murray, "Be careful who you choose as your friends. I'd rather have four quarters than a hundred pennies." Every year I add a few more silver dollars to my pockets, for which I am always grateful.

For their abundant love, support, and encouragement, my thanks as always to my wonderful family, especially my parents, Mike and Judy Scarsbrook.

And, as always, this book is for Bluebell, my love, my muse, and my best friend. For evermore.

ALSO BY RICHARD SCARSBROOK

The Indifference League

Sexy, racy, hilarious, and even moving, *The Indifference League* is a story of what happens when the starry-eyed optimism of the Greatest Generation crashes into the obsessions and fears of the New Lost Generation. Under the faded banner of Superman, Wonder Woman, and other heroes past, steps the Indifference League: The Statistician, Time Bomb, Hippie Avenger, SuperKen, SuperBarbie, Miss Demeanor, Mr. Nice Guy, Psycho Superstar, The Drifter, and The Stunner. All archetypes of Generations X and Y, they are here to show us just how much things have changed. Sex and love. Religion and politics. Left and Right. Right and Wrong. Can anyone be a hero in an age where the lines are so blurred? When they meet again at The Hall of Indifference for a long weekend together, The Indifference League will fight to find out. Or not.

MORE FICTION FROM DUNDURN

Festival Man
Geoff Berner

Travel in the entertaining company of a man made of equal parts bullshit and inspiration, in what is ultimately a twisted panegyric to the power of strange music to change people from the inside out. At turns funny and strangely sobering, this "found memoir" is a picaresque tale of inspired, heroic deceit, incompetence, and — just possibly — triumph. Follow the flailing escapades of maverick music manager Campbell Ouiniette at the Calgary Folk Festival, as he leaves a trail of empty liquor bottles, cigarette butts, bruised egos, and obliterated relationships behind him. His top headlining act has abandoned him for the Big Time. In a fit of self-delusion or pure genius (or perhaps a bit of both), Ouiniette devises an intricate scam, a last hurrah in an attempt to redeem himself in the eyes of his girlfriend, the music industry, and the rest of the world. He reveals his path of destruction in his own transparently self-justifying, explosive, profane words, with digressions into the Edmonton hardcore punk rock scene, the Yugoslavian Civil War, and other epicentres of chaos.